# Bad Elf

# and

# The Krampus

A Twisted Christmas Tale

JOHN RAE

ISBN-13: 979-8-9865397-8-2

For Emma.

# AUTHOR'S NOTE

*Bad Elf and The Krampus* is an updated version of *Bad Elf*. Some characters and scenes were changed and added in order to create a foundation for a larger story.

# Table of Contents


Author's Note............................................................4

1 - Christmas Canceled! ...................................6

2 - Un. Can. Cel. ...........................................21

3 - Reindeer Games ....................................38

4 - Perma-swear.........................................53

5 - Happy Christmas Eve! ..........................71

6 - The Trouble With Being Santa ...............79

7 - Lame!..................................................93

8 - Elf On The Frigging Shelf!....................106

9 - Secret Santa .......................................112

10 – Careful What You Wish For ..............122

11 - Dunkelstimma ...................................134

12 - Letters To Santa................................143

13 – A Slippery Slope................................150

14 - Make Like An Elf ...............................163

15 - Battle!...............................................171

16 – Santa's Secret ..................................199

17 – One Christmas Wish .........................224

About The Author.....................................229

Cover Art .................................................230

Preview ...................................................231

One Last Wish..........................................244

# 1 - CHRISTMAS CANCELED!

Holy hell, it's cold!

That's about all Jackie Rumpus might have to say about life at The Pole, except that it is also dark and dreary. And muted. And desolate—with a bitter and biting swirling wind. You won't find it on any map, but The Pole is a snowy campus nestled in the valley between seven mountains known collectively as The Crown. The path into this world tucks between a gap between the Crown's tines…where legend says an eighth mountain once stood but was stolen. Can you believe that? A mountain…stolen? Even if you could steal a mountain, what good would stealing one do?

Anywho…The Pole, of course, has more to it than cold and mountains. The campus itself mixes new buildings and old, fantastic cottages. And, of course, it also has reindeer—housed in a small, red and weathered barn way off campus because, let's face it, reindeer stink. And in such a place where *downwind* happens to be in just about every direction, it is best to keep the beasts away.

And, of course, The Pole has Santa Claus, whose familiar black boots crunched through the snow to the reindeer barn to spend a few minutes of his day with his oldest friends—Dasher, Dancer, Prancer, Vixen, Comet, Cupid, Donner, and Blitzen. Oh! And Rudolph. We can't forget Rudy. Santa's team. They had been with Santa on many Christmas Eve adventures and even more less-Christmasy adventures. Often, it took just a few moments, checking in with them to calm Santa from an otherwise crabby day. Today was one of those crabby days. Come to think of it, most days lately have been crabby days, with Santa holed up in his corner office at North Pole Headquarters, fumbling over a problem he couldn't quite place. Something troubled him, but Santa couldn't figure out what. And unfortunately for Santa, today's visit with his team would offer no relief from said crabbiness…it would make it only worse. But it just might help expose what was troubling him.

He reached the small barn, creaked open the doors, and flipped a set of those old-timey knife switches—the kind that spark and smell of ozone when thrown—and a series of lights flickered brighter, illuminating row after row of reindeer pens, several stories high. Now, you might wonder how so many reindeer could fit inside such a tiny, old barn, but things at The Pole aren't always what they seem. For in addition to cold, reindeer, and Santa, The Pole had magic. Polar Magic.

"Boys and girls!" Santa called. The reindeer met his greeting with braying and lowing, grunting. A few elves working in the humid space called back a round of hellos before returning to their work. The pens closest to the doors held his team, and each was marked with an ancient and weathered wooden nameplate, painted with flaking gold and red paint in the long, scrolling lettering the elves fancied. As Santa stepped over to the pen with Blitzen's nameplate, he tripped on a small, tan, saddle that some rogue elf had forgotten to put away. "Son of a-" he winced, catching his words before tumbling down with a strained "ho…ho…ho."

A concerned red glow brightened from Rudolph's pen. Santa's leg had bent at just the wrong place! Bent at just the wrong angle! Not merely sprained or strained, but clearly broke. And so very close to Christmas Eve. Santa winced, less from pain and more out of frustration, as he slammed the saddle against the pen. He stared where it fell as a few stable elves rushed over. And try as they might to help him, Santa shushed them away, assuring them that he was fine. More than fine. The best ever, in fact!

"Clearly not fine," one of the stable elves mumbled as they went back to work.

"Ya think?" another replied, glancing back at the old man. "You know who forgot to put the saddle away?"

The first elf shook his head, startled when Santa groaned to his feet. Santa's famous *A-merry-Christmas-to-all-and-to-all-a-good-night!* shout was a mere casual greeting in comparison to this groan. Sounded as if his very soul had fled from his body. Santa grabbed a tiny shovel and snatched the saddle before hobbling back out into the cold, grunting with each step.

Several minutes later, he staggered into the bright-white infirmary…the Elf Hospital tucked neatly in the corner of Headquarters. With every step, he winced and grumped, leaning on that shovel that smelled like the parting end of a reindeer. The nurse elf took his shovel and led Santa past the large central fireplace, past rows of mostly-empty elf-sized beds to one of the two grown-human-sized beds that rarely ever saw use. Now, you might be wondering on the size of an elf-sized bed. Well, most elves would come up to just over Santa's knee, and the nurse elf was no different. She grunted under the weight of Santa's hobbling, for he leaned his entire weight onto her cap—a regular flip-front nurse cap that Santa had smushed, and whose top draped down the back in a long, candy-striped stocking. Her bright-white uniform refused to let go of a few cherry-colored stains from patients suffering from the Sugarplum Trinkles over the years. "Oof!" she grunted, the bell on the end of her cap rattling with each step until The Missus rushed in and took her husband's weight.

"It's broke," Santa grumbled towards the bed. "Tripped over a saddle." His frustration sneaked away from him in the way he enunciated *saddle*, baring his teeth.

The Missus sat next to him on the bed and let the nurse inspect the leg. "I tell ya, if you're going to go joy-riding you should bring someone to help." She rubbed his back. "For moments like this!"

"I wasn't riding. Just visiting. It was one of the elves. Left the saddle on the floor. Probably left in a hurry because they were riding one of my team." The nurse and The Missus gasped. "I know, right? How many times do I warn them that nobody rides Santa's team except Santa?" He grunted but then howled in pain as sparks fizzled from the nurse's hands over his leg and broken bones crunched and twisted back into place.

"Well, that will set it," she said. "But I still need to put it in a cast."

"Snowballs," Santa groaned, folding his arms across his chest.

The Missus watched him pout. "What can you do?" she finally asked. "Can't just cancel Christmas."

Santa turned an eye on her…now there was an idea. "I'm so annoyed right now. I don't feel very Christmasy."

"Nonsense, dear. You haven't been very Christmasy all year." On his sharp glance, she added, "Just saying. If we followed the Chinese calendar, this would be the Year of The Crab. Not that they traditionally have Crab Years, mind you."

"You're not very comforting."

"You've been such a crab-butt, I think your hinder just might be forming an exoskeleton," she smiled with a wink. It was a subtle smile and an equally subtle wink, but they had the most not-so-subtle effect on melting Santa's heart. She always made him grin. And once he did so, she leaned into him for a hug as the nurse wrapped his leg. "I'm sorry you broke your leg. And I'm sorry for whatever it is that's been troubling you. I wish you would talk to me about it."

"I wish I knew what *it* was." And this was no lie, for the amount of time he spent trying to figure it out had grown from hours to days, to weeks and then months. He'd sit at his desk, staring at his computer screen, sometimes crushing candy, sometimes distracting himself with social media and finding whose Instapic snapshots might warrant inclusion on the Naughty List. And though it looked like he might just be goofing off, he was always wondering what to do about *something*.

*But what was that thing?*

The Missus watched him think with some suspicion that finally gave way to giving him the benefit of the doubt. If he actually knew what was bothering him, he had always been the kind of elf who would do something about it. "Do you know who's been riding your team?"

"I've my suspicions. The question is…" He trailed off, nodding his forefinger against his nose. "What to do about it?"

And that question brought a twinkle to his eye, for The Missus was right about him. If there was something to do, he would do it. The gears in his head cranked and turned, and spun together a plan.

By all accounts, the factory floor of the Toy Shoppe was a happy sweatshop—bright, colorful, warm— where row after row of festive elves worked tirelessly at their workstations, making toys, and singing along to holiday music. They moved at a feverish pace, to you and me, zipping along with their hand tools and such…but to them, their pace seemed pretty normal.

But then there was Jack, who hardly moved at all. As a matter of fact, if Jack could not move at all, he'd be not moving at a feverish elf-pace. But, of course, he couldn't not move *at all*, certainly not with the angry music blasting in his earbuds. He sat on his work stool, bopping along and tapping a candy-striped ring against the tabletop of his workstation. In his early twenties, Jack had reached the point in his life where even though he wasn't quite an adult elf, he was expected to be, well, more adult-like. Like Santa, he felt stuck. But, unlike Santa, Jack knew what his problem was, and he knew what he needed to do. He needed a change. As he tapped that ring to the music, he fantasized about what he planned to do.

His eyes, circled by dark eyeliner, stared off into space under a curly mop of jet-black-dyed hair. He wore a pale makeup to hide the natural rosiness of his cheeks, but he looked as dark and cold as the outside. The fake piercings and intentionally-torn clothes were Jack's way of saying, "If you're going to look at me, don't look at *me*." Folks at The Pole didn't know what to make of him. He was restless, bored, angry, a loner, weird, and well, very un-elf-like.

Even the things that made him happy and excitable were odd. Most all the elves, for example, idolized Santa. But not Jack. He idolized Krampus. Like some rock-star roadie, across the back of his red work vest, Jack had dramatically etched his idol's name. And who is Krampus? A demon. A Christmas demon. A demon whose job is to punish the naughtiest of children on Christmas Eve.

But there was something else that made Jack happy and excitable…Candi Kane. Candi was more like your stereotypical, bright-eyed, elf. A stark contrast to Jack, the only hint of darkness in her was her necklace pendant—a jack o' lantern bat, made festive with a Santa hat. Her long, blonde bob had a shock of pink in the bangs today—a dash of color that often reflected her mood. "Jackie!" she shouted, yanking out his earbuds and startling him from his daydream.

"Gah! What?" He quickly put the candy-striped ring on his middle finger.

"Don't you want to win the contest?" She pointed to the factory wall, to a large poster that showed a happy elf riding alongside Santa on a snowy night, delivering presents. It read:

### RIDE WITH SANTA!

Jack turned to his small stack of half-baked, pathetic toys. A few were truly inspired but with Jack's own dark twist. His latest doll, for example, was of a bride. A corpse-bride. Emptiness peered out from her button eyes; empty, yet thoughtful; as if her mind twisted upon itself every bit as much as the horns that spiraled out from her head. Jack picked her up and admired that dark gaze. "Nope," he said as if the answer to Candi's question should be obvious. Why *would* he want to ride with Santa?

Just then, Santa charged into the factory on the catwalk overlooking the elves. Sporting his leg cast, he thumped along with a cane, which he whacked against the railing to command attention. Here, in front of the elves, it was easier to see he was not the jolly, fat elf we expect. Instead, he was more of a grumpy dad. Towering over the elves, he grunted in disgust, throwing down the saddle over which he had tripped. Work stopped as everyone gave him their curious attention. Eying Jack, Santa grumbled, "Someone has been sneaking Rudolph out for a joyride! How many times do I have to tell you that nobody flies Santa's team, but Santa?" A collective gasp from the elves nearly sucked the air from the room. Candi turned to Jack, wide-eyed. Jack mouthed that it wasn't him. "The Missus says, and The Missus is right...Christmas is canceled!"

Heartbroken, the elves all mumbled and groaned, turning to one another...surprised and confused. But, astonishingly, nobody was more upset than Jack. He kicked at the table leg and marched straight up to Santa, bounding up the stacked presents on up to the catwalk, coming nearly face-to-kneecap. The rosiness of his cheeks burned, shining through the makeup. "Rumplemints!" He stomped his foot. "You can't just *cancel* Christmas!"

"Language, Rumpus." Santa shot Jack a very dad-like warning glare. But it was more than just a dad-like warning glare. Once the frown gave way to an arched right eyebrow, a sigh escaped Santa's lips, his head cocked just slightly askew, and his left cheek pulled in a slight twist, the warning glare had finished morphing into what the elves called *The Santa Look*. And it was an annoyed, somewhat pained, look that was used almost exclusively for Jack.

Jack breathed heavy as they stared down one another until finally, Jack broke. "Christmas ain't yours to cancel." Everyone turned on Jack...un-be-lievable. And the leers and jeers didn't end as their shift suddenly ended and the elves all made their way back to their dorms. All through the crowded hall, elves bumped him, nudged him, poked him and did what he hated most...they looked at him, with glaring eyes, of course, all giving him grief for getting Christmas canceled. Candi did her best to chase after him.

"Way to go, Snowflake!" Feliz snapped, just as he pushed Jack up against the wall and held him there. What Feliz lacked in height, he made up for in stockiness…unusual in both, in regards to an elf.

Feliz's taller-and-skinnier-than-usual crony, Mickie, chimed in. "I busted my jingle bells trying to win that contest!" Mickie's elf hat flipped forward from him snapping his neck so hard with anger.

Jack remained calm. "I didn't cancel Christmas."

"Why do you hang around this loser?" Feliz snapped at Candi—who tugged at his arm to get him off Jack. His *loser* comment didn't bother Jack at all, but when Feliz bumped Candi away, he totally lost his cool. Jack grunted, kicked forward and slammed Feliz against the opposite wall.

"You gotta problem with me? Fine!" he snarled. "You don't touch Candi."

And now Candi tugged at Jack's arm, flustered in trying to calm everyone down. "It's all right, Jackie!"

"It's Jack!" he shouted, before releasing Feliz.

Feliz adjusted the collar on his workshop vest, watching Jack walk away before finally hissing just loud enough, "Freak!"

"Feliz…" Jack stopped, and stomped back to Feliz. "We live at The Pole. We dress like this. Make toys so that some jolly guy can deliver them on to people who put weirdly-decorated trees in their living rooms. Trees! In their living rooms!" Jack shook his head. "You ever think we might all be freaks?" He stared into Feliz's empty expression for a moment before storming away.

Candi paused in his wake, sighing, before catching up to Jack. "I don't understand you, Jackie. Why do you hate Santa so much?"

"I don't hate him," he shrugged, pushing through the crowd.

Jack reached his room. The nameplate on his door had been marked up so that JACKIE RUMPUS now read JACK KRUMPUS. His own Goth scribbles flourished across his door—flying skulls, lurking ghosts, strange fantastical creatures that came from his imagination— like a patched and stitched-up rag-doll puppy with deep, hollow, eyes and a flaming tail—and, of course, a doodle of his idol, Krampus. In addition to those doodles, vandals had marked his door with very un- Christmasy words and images. *Freak*, *Loser*, and *#Snowflake* peppered depictions such as Jack getting run over by a reindeer. Jack never bothered to remove the vandalism, for he found the irony of their hate juxtaposed with anti-Christmas sentiments slightly homey. Nobody ever understood his joke. Except maybe for Candi, who lately seemed more and more lost on the irony.

Candi caught up to him again. "Then why do you act like you hate Santa? Or care if Christmas is canceled?"

Jack twisted with a pointed finger. "Every year we get a single Christmas wish. Just one!" As he turned back to fuss with the lock, "I have the same wish every year. To meet Krampus. And fat man never comes through. Never." He looked Candi in the eye to make his point. "Santa. Hates. Me." He opened the door to illuminate the dark room, exposing more darkness, even after he turned on the lights. Posters of Goth bands like The

Steamed PUnKs wallpapered the tiny room, along with vintage-looking posters for Krampus. *Greetings from the Krampus*, read one poster—showing a horned devil with rather playful eyes. *The Christmas Demon*, read another—showing a shadow of a tall horned figure with one human leg and one goat leg, hauling a basket full of children over his shoulder. Another *The Devil of Christmas* showed a horned Krampus behaving rather naughty with a scantily-clad woman. *Krampusnacht* showed him as white and furry, different from the others that showed him as black and hairy. And finally, Jack's favorite poster showed a threatening Krampus, towering over frightened and cowering children. Very prominently, it read:

*You've Been Naughty!*

Candi looked about his otherwise oddly empty room with some suspicion and then back to the Krampus posters. "How can Santa deliver something that isn't real?"

"Krampus is *so* real."

"A story moms and dads use to trick kids into behaving for Christmas."

Jack raised an eyebrow. "Like Santa Claus?"

"Except Santa is real."

Jack slumped into a chair and pouted. "Why can't I just have something to believe in?"

Candi teased with a little sing-song jab. "You better not pout."

Jack glared up at her…not in the mood. He took off his ridiculous elf shoes. The tiny bell on the end of each was made up with devil horns, which not only paid homage to Jack's idol but also muted their twinkling and jingling into a dull rattle. "I need Christmas uncanceled."

"I don't understand you, Jackie." She watched him stretch his toes in his striped stockings and felt a huge distance between the two of them. "We used to be best friends."

Jack frowned, and looked up to her, confused. "We're friends." How could Candi feel otherwise? She was his only friend at The Pole, let alone his *best* friend.

Candi looked at all the posters. "We're in different worlds."

"Right!" Jack sat up. "I don't belong here, Candi. You're the only one who can't see it. I hate The Pole. I hate making toys. I hate red. And green. And I hate our stupid elf names. And-"

"You hate my name?" The lump in her throat hardly hid the hurt, giving her voice a slight gravel.

Jack rattled off names as if counting them on his fingers. "Jackie Rumpus. Candi Kane. Feliz Navidad. Holly Pumpernickel. Mickie Rooney." He shook his head. "And everyone thinks I'm nuts because I want to be just Jack."

Up with the air quotes. "Jack '*Krumpus*.'"

"So?"

Feeling like the distance might be just too great for her to handle in that moment, Candi turned to leave…and tripped over the opening for a Santa sack that stuck out from under the bed. Jack spun in his seat, their eyes locking for a moment as a secret had just revealed itself. She snatched up the sack and dumped its contents onto the floor—and the room that had been oddly empty became suddenly un-oddly empty. Goth knickknacks, elf hats, his first wooden toy-making mallet, Jack's favorite pillow, his first toy robot, a picture of him and Candi as children—enjoying a laugh at Hollyberry Farms under the Northern Lights—a seemingly endless pile of Jack's belongings spilled out—more so than could possibly fit inside the bag. Yet, even so, after Candi gave the bag one final shake, and a tiny pair of underpants tumbled out, the sack still appeared to be filled with toys. Candi stood a moment, eyes thoughtful as she reached for Jack's favorite steampunk goggles. She rubbed her thumb against its dark blue lens as her eyes grew less thoughtful and more angry, fixing on Jack. Finally, she whipped the sack at him, which collapsed flat when it hit. "Going somewhere, Jackie?"

Jack stared at the truck heap, thinking, before finally confessing, "I'm running away from The Pole. Christmas Eve. While he's away delivering presents."

Candi rolled her eyes, hurt that he wouldn't share this with her. Intentionally at least. How it started to hurt her to even speak. "Where would you even go?"

"I'm gonna go live with Krampus."

She shook her head…you're nuts. "He's not real."

"He is," Jack insisted. "And I think, maybe-" He trailed off to find the right words. Something that would help her understand. "Maybe I just *belong* on a darker side of Christmas."

Her frustration escalated with each word. "He's. Not. Real!" She took another look at the posters of his idol. "And even if he were, Jackie, Krampus is evil."

"He's not evil!" Jack shot to his feet. "He just doesn't waste any time on the good kids. Only worries about the bad." Candi glared, unconvinced. "He and Santa used to even ride together! But now Santa does both jobs and just gives bad kids a lump of coal. Whoop-de-do. And most of the time, he doesn't even bother doing that much." He thought a moment. "He's a little too stingy with the coal if you ask me."

As if saying as much would show him the absurdity of what he believed, Candi sighed. "Meanwhile, Krampus drags them to Hell in a handbasket."

But this only got Jack excited. "I know, right?!"

Candi huffed, and shook her head, feeling lost and overwhelmed by that distance between them. Like the Santa sack, that small space between them felt full of extra space, stuffed with something that seemed unnecessary and yet desperately needed. But all Candi could do in the moment was to let that distance (and Jack) just be.

# 2 - UN. CAN. CEL.

The reason you won't find The Pole—or The Crown, for that matter—on any map, is that it is protected by Polar Magic. As if encased within a giant snow globe, an invisible border lightly shimmers with the Northern Lights if someone who doesn't belong attempts to trek inside. Imagine you and a friend attempted the frigid journey north and made it to the border. Another step from you would send you clear to the other side of The Crown, and you wouldn't know what had happened. If you were then to turn back to your friend, you might be able to discern them in the very far distance, provided the weather was bright and sunshiny, which is rarely ever the case at The Pole. And in the distance between you and your friend, you wouldn't see The Pole, nor would you see the seven tines of The Crown. You'd just see the gap between you, and think one of you had gotten lost in the snow. But you certainly wouldn't ever know that Santa was near, for at The Pole there are only two types of people…those who belong there, and those who are invited.

And this fact was a huge deal for Jack, for he never knew to which group he belonged. Not much about

The Pole felt inviting, and very little gave him a sense of belonging there.

There are many types of magical creatures and several types of elves in the world. The Woodland Elves, for example, are stewards of forests and keepers of the dark. And, yes, the darkness must be kept. Zephyr Elves live in the clouds, and are more popularly known as Faeries…but don't ever call them that to their face. Never, ever, ever. The term is considered not-so-politically correct. Zephyrs bring messages and battle with storms. Tinchers, often considered evil, are actually no more or less evil than Zephyrs, but they move through fire and their rage can be difficult to manage. The Toy Elves at The Pole are more properly known as Phantagrasons. They build things, are problem solvers, and they move really, really fast—zipping about in what seems like a normal fashion for them. Their creative drive makes them perfect for making toys, however, Phantagrasons lack direction. Tell a typical Toy Elf to make a stuffed animal, for example, and their most creative spark turns into a child's amusement. But don't tell a Phantagrason to make a stuffed animal, and the elf may sit idly—frustrated perhaps because they feel like they should be doing something, but unsure what it is they should do. And that is where Santa comes in. He directs them, plans for them, takes care of them, and gives them focus that every day should be the next Christmas Eve and their reward of happy children all the world over…for a happy child most definitely is their kind of magic.

And Jack…he had drive. And this set him apart from all the other elves; further apart than his makeup and clothes and such had already set him apart. He didn't particularly like all the things that Phantagrasons liked. He rarely seemed happy. But there was something else that set Jack apart from the others, and it was actually something he had in common with them. Nobody really knew if Jack belonged at The Pole, or if he had been invited.

Elves aren't magically hatched into the world…they have parents just the same as you and I, but Jack was also an orphan. Those in the know didn't know much of anything other than one day a baby Jack just showed up. And the question was…did he belong there, or was he invited? Santa hadn't much to say about the situation other than to tell folks to mind their own business. That, of course, Jack belonged there. The Pole was his home.

But Jack never did like what the other elves liked. He was too tall to be a Faerie, yet figurative storms brooded about him. The darkness suggested Woodland…but Jack was a million times too short to be a Woodland Elf. The passion and rage suggested maybe Tincher…if you were to squint just right. He seemed to be a Toy Elf, but he also seemed to be something else, too. Only Santa knew for sure, maybe, and Santa wasn't talking…not even to Jack, who had asked the question once or twice. Santa would always reiterate that The Pole was his home, knowing full well that that wasn't really what Jack was asking. So still, Jack's question loomed…did he belong there, or was he invited?

On a normal day, Jack took a bit of time to get ready. After all, it took effort to put on his makeup, add the trinkets to his eyes, nose, and ears, and have his clothes torn just right to create the illusion of not caring. But today was not normal and he needed to create the illusion of caring.

Gone was the makeup that made his face pale. Gone was the eyeliner that made his eyes deathly serious. Gone were the trinkets that made it so his face looked full of holes. Gone were the torn clothes. Rather than putting on regular everyday elf clothes, however, Jack put on his best outfit—a black suit and tie he hadn't worn since some ancient funeral. The mirror reflected a proper elf, and as Jack mustered up the courage to do what he had to do, he kept finding reasons to procrastinate. Like the black mop atop his head. Unruly. Very Rumpus-like. He combed it down, re-wetting it and re-gelling it, over and over and over again, but he could not get it to look serious enough. It seemed as if he might be able to get it just right, only to have a hair or two out of place, but by the time he fought those hairs into place, the mop had sprung back into existence.

"Crumpets!"

A knock on the door was a welcomed relief. Candi was already in the middle of a sentence by the time he opened the door and she had got a good look at him. "Well," she paused, with a smile. "Look at you!"

Jack's eyebrows arched, noticing the pink shock in her hair was crimson today, and he wondered what that meant. If it meant anything at all. "What's wrong with me?"

"Nothing," she said, adjusting his tie. "Did someone die?"

He shook his head. "I have to go and see Santa. Gotta get Christmas uncanceled."

Candi frowned. Her hand dropped from his tie. "So you can run away?" Jack nodded. "I was going to see if you wanted to get breakfast, but you got plans." She turned away.

"Maybe afterwards?" he jumped. "I can come get you."

Candi turned back to Jack's smile. And his smile made her smile. She caressed his bare cheek with the back of her hand, causing Jack's face to twist up in question. "It's been a long while since I've seen you without all that crap on."

"I like that crap."

"I know you do. I had forgotten how soft your eyes could look." Her gaze hovered on his for a moment before she turned away. "Breakfast when you're done." Jack watched her long, blonde bob sway as she sprited away, his hand touching his cheek where she left him. He knew she was hurting, but he was hurting, too. And now, that hurt seemed to tumble into something else he couldn't quite place. He would miss her. Terribly.

Bright-eyed and curious, Jack walked through the wide office space of North Pole Headquarters, making his way to a large corner office where the nameplate read S. CLAUS. He paused for courage, looking about the cube farm and wondering what it would be like to work there instead of at the Toy Shoppe. And what did the elves who worked at HQ even do? Probably had something to do with reading Letters to Santa. And maintaining the Naughty and Nice lists. Maybe something to do with getting supplies for all the toys they made? He finally turned away from the office staff and knocked at the door. No answer. Knocked again and waited. And when it was clear that nobody was inside, he opened the door using a second, much lower doorknob placed just for the elves and peered in.

Jack had already snuck inside before giving any thought to whether it was naughty or nice to simply let himself in. The obnoxiously long office struck him with awe. More corporate than festive, yet definitely Santa's personal space. As he snuck about, Jack gawked at everything—twenty-foot-high bookshelves crammed with every Christmas story ever written, along with a few non-Christmas books from Santa's favorite authors. "Old Man and the Sea," he read, running his fingers along the book spines, and wondering just who was Earnest Hemmingway, or Mark Twain. He pulled out a book by a Stephen King. "Ooh! This looks like fun," he said, reading the back cover. "And…really, really scary," he added, putting the book back as if the demons it contained might spill out and into the chill shimmering down his spine.

A large telescope, oddly fixed on some space in the very far distance, took center stage on the wide bay windows that overlooked the campus. Jack closed an eye and peered into the eyepiece. He could make out a mountain standing tall behind a curtain of harsh snow. He straightened up and looked out with the naked eye…couldn't see anything. Another peer into the eyepiece and he thought he could make out a cave entrance high towards the mountaintop. He straightened up again and squinted into the distance. Nothing. "Weird."

Even weirder, he thought, were the strange trinkets scattered about. Mostly steampunk in design, with gears and springs and twisted metal…Jack grinned at them all, wondering what they were all about. Perhaps he and Santa had a little more in common than he thought? He picked up a small wreath of sorts, made up of eight old gears, tarnished and gritty. Across seven of the gears were keys, equally ancient, attached at the bits and bent slightly towards the center of the ring where their decorative and incredibly ornate bows stretched towards one another, but wouldn't ever quite touch. Jack picked up the wreath by the gear without a key. It felt weirdly heavy, much heavier than it should, yet somehow delicate; like if he weren't too careful, he might snap off a key. To Jack's surprise, the wreath began to vibrate as the empty gear turned between his fingers. The surprise of the motion caused Jack to drop the wreath, which fell back to the table and wobbled with a grinding noise. His gasp gave way to a shushing, pleading for the spinning wreath to quiet and please, please, please don't break. He frantically shushed, eyes darting between the door and the metal ring that rattled like a spinning coin that finally lost its momentum to a full and quiet stop.

"Whew!" Jack breathed, waiting a moment to see if the noise had grabbed anyone's attention. "Okay," he finally said to himself. "Try not to touch anything." But, of course, this was Jack, who couldn't help but run his hand along the many, many Santa hats that were scattered about—and not just the style we're familiar with, with the fuzzy white brim and poof ball. A formal red top hat, trimmed with hollyberry, rested atop a coat rack. Santa's favorite whimsical ones—like the ones that looked like a reindeer, or made with a silly spring—

usually given to him as gifts from children—lined one of the walls with colorful, pointed Christmas hats and droopy red hoods, and old ornately decorated religious caps—like a red velvet bowl cap, embroidered with fine gold silk in patterns that radiated outward from its green center puff ball. The patterns matched the different bows of the key wreath and gave a clue to what the missing key might look like—sort of like a path that had forked, where the tines bent off into more forks and further forks. "That would make for a really complicated key," Jack thought, continuing on to what struck him as the strangest Santa hat of them all. An ancient, pale green and red elf hat with brushed nickel bells, resting by itself on a small stand near Santa's desk. It wasn't just the style that made it an elf hat, but its tiny size.

As he reached for the hat, a motion caught in the corner of his eye yanked his attention—ephemeral fog swirling inside a snow globe larger than Jack. It entranced him, as if the fog reached out to him like a hand and pulled him gently close. As he ran his fingers over the glass, the swirls glowed and bended to his touch. Something hid inside the mist, and Jack tried to bend the swirls out of his way so he could see whatever it was inside the glass, but he decided to give up the hunt as it continued to elude him.

Jack turned towards Santa's desk and climbed into the large office chair. He was ridiculously small in the seat, but his beaming smile made up for his lack of size. He pushed against the desk, trying to spin the chair, until his gaze landed on something that finally looked expected yet still surprising. How his eyes grew!

"The Naughty List!" he gasped. A post-it attached to the scroll read *Check this twice. Love, The Missus.*

"Rumpus!" Santa bellowed from the door. Jack yelped, jumped up and in his surprise, yanked the Naughty List and other bric-a-brac from the desktop into a scattering heap at his feet. When the papers all settled he peered from behind the desk to find that Santa had already zipped all the way to the desk, and was crouched down and peering right back at Jack. "What are you doing in my office?"

"Looking for you, sir," Jack tried in his most sincere-sounding tone that didn't fool Santa a bit.

"Sir?" Santa huffed, unimpressed.

"You can't cancel Christmas."

"Because it is not mine to cancel, I presume?" Santa's eyebrows raised in a question...are we having this conversation again?

"I-I'm sorry about that," Jack flustered. "I was angry. Shocked! Christmas canceled?"

Santa was slightly amused at the air quotes Jack had put up around the word *canceled.* He towered up tall, tapping his cane against his cast. "Look at me, Jackie. My leg is broken." Jack tried his doe-y-est doe eyes and suggested that he could deliver presents for Santa. "Right," Santa chuckled. "Jackie Rumpus as Santa. Plan B." Santa's deep hee-hee-hee's gradually morphed into a hysterical ho-ho-ho, driving a hurt Jack from the office.

But as Jack shut the door behind him, he realized it wasn't hurt he felt, for he never really expected Santa to warm up to the idea of Jack delivering presents Christmas Eve. Still, the ho-ho-ho's from the other side of the door zinged a little bit. "Plan B?" he thought. No, it wasn't hurt he felt at all. He felt *challenged*.

At breakfast, his new—but definitely going to be short-lived—look caught everyone's attention. And as he and Candi made their way through the food lines to the tables, the elves all did what Jack hated most…they looked at him. How he wished he had gone back to his room to first take off this costume.

"Who died?" asked Feliz, attempting to trip Jack. But even though Jack couldn't see Feliz's foot while carrying his tray of food, Jack had enough experience to know he needed to take an off-step to avoid tumbling. He tried to conjure a witty comeback, but his insecurities muddled his wit bit, and so he decided that ignoring Feliz might instead be the best decision. He and Candi sat down to breakfast where he gave her all the details about how things went not-so-well with Santa.

"I need a Plan B," he finally said.

"What's Plan B?" Candi asked, dripping hot maple syrup over her pancakes.

Jack shrugged. "Gotta figure that out yet." Just then, Jack was hit in the face with a cold serving of grits. The white, buttery cornmeal dripped from his face. He wiped it from his eyes and was met with laughter from Feliz and Mickie.

"Not funny, Rooney!" Candi snapped, and as she leaned forward like she meant to launch a full-on food fight, Jack caught her arm in his hand. He gently shook his head. She looked into his eyes, fire gone…what's wrong?

"You forgot your clownface," Feliz laughed.

Jack stood, strangely calm, but with a forced calm that readied to explode. "The difference between my clownface and yours, Feliz, is that I can wash mine away."

Feliz jumped up and lunged towards Jack, only to be blocked by Candi—who tripped him and then rolled him over her foot so he landed on his back. "Not today!" she snapped with a finger jabbed into his chest.

"Let's just get out of here, Candi," Jack nudged.

And as they walked away, Feliz shouted, "Need your girlfriend to fight your battles?"

Candi started to turn back. "I'm not his-" Jack yanked her arm, tugging her along.

"You're right," Jack said. "Not today. Whatever Plan B is, I'm pretty sure it requires me being on my best behavior. Santa wouldn't listen to me otherwise."

"You can't let him bully you like that."

"And how often do I let him?" Jack smirked. Candi frowned…you're right. "But thanks for sticking up for me."

"Jolly Dead Brigade, right?" she smiled. "Always got each other's backs." The Jolly Dead Brigade was their private joke. Their private club! Something they created for just the two of them when they were elflings.

On their walk back to the dorms, Jack excused himself to the restroom so as to get the grits out of his ear. Under the fluorescent lights at the sink, he washed his face, washed out his ear, and by the time he was done drying himself off, the mop atop his head was even moppier. He took a good look at himself. "Clownface?" he sniffled. He felt absurdly naked out and about like this.

Candi and Jack crossed the walkway that connected North Pole Headquarters with the older dormitory, briefly pausing to watch the traffic pass beneath them…mostly reindeer-drawn sleds, snowmobiles, and Kettlekarts—fully automated vehicles that kept the passengers warm around a central fireplace that fueled the ride itself. Kettlekarts were imbued with the same Polar Magic as the Santa sack—they were much larger on the inside than seemingly possible. Jack always thought they looked more like rum jugs rather than kettles—like fat bottles that curved around the central chimney. Elves rushed from the buildings and darted between the cars, bringing traffic to a stop as everyone pointed towards HQ and shouted the news to one another. More and more elves poured into the streets, looking up to a large digital billboard in the city center, anxiously anticipating a message from Santa.

Jack questioned Candi with a look…what's going on? And then, from around the corner of the dormitory hall, the street's commotion had spread. "Christmas has been uncanceled!" someone shouted. Candi's eyes grew wide, and Jack…he hadn't time enough to protest his innocence from having done some *thing* before darting off towards the excitement, to where excited elves crowded about. Candi and Jack pushed their way through the ruckus to a *RIDE WITH SANTA!* poster, only now it read:

*CHRISTMAS UNCANCELED!*
*RIDE FOR SANTA!*

Candi lamented Jack's excitement. But, of course, he would be excited. He snatched the candy cane marker to sign-up. "What do you think you're doing?" Mickie snarled.

"Got as much chance as you," Jack snapped, scribbling his name.

Mickie's simple "Ha!" retort wasn't even a jab. That Jackie Rumpus could think that Santa would ever even consider him for the job felt truly ridiculous.

But then Candi went and did something that not only surprised her but shocked Jack. She took the marker and signed up, too! "Uh, Candi?"

"There's no chance Santa will pick you before me!" she said.

"What?!" That zinged more than Mickie's *Ha!* Jack yanked the marker away and scribbled off her name.

"You can't do that!" She snatched the marker back.

"Hey!" And with that, Plan B's obvious requirement for best behavior was shot, for they fought over the marker, yelling like children, both scribbling off the other's name and writing down their own each time they controlled the marker. Fully entertained, the elves cheered, until…Santa arrived.

"What the devil is going on here?" he shouted. He leaned on his cane, hunched over for being nearly too big for the hall. The elves all scattered so that only Jack and Candi remained, each with a hand on the marker and the scribbled-up poster that had frayed up a bit at the edges. They looked to one another, surprised at how much they had marked up the other; Jack was particularly horrified that he had ditched Plan B in such spectacular fashion in front of the very person he desperately wanted to impress.

"Ride *for* Santa?" Santa huffed, gob-smacked as anyone at this development. He ripped the poster from the wall and charged away, whacking his cane against a garbage can that had made the unfortunate mistake of being in his way. Jack and Candi frowned at one another, forgot what they were fighting about, and then chased after Santa back to the Toy Shoppe where rows of elves worked diligently now that it appeared that Christmas had been, in fact, uncanceled.

In the corner, in a creaking rocking chair, sat Crusty. He stood strangely about twice as tall as other elves, thin and bent with age, sporting a long wispy white beard. Teaching the young elves how to make basic wooden toys, he inspected the clacker on a clickety-clack train and helped its elfling maker tweak it to clack even louder. When Santa barged in on the catwalk and rapped his cane against the railing, all work stopped, and Santa's ruckus was loud enough to startle even Crusty…who couldn't hear well at all. He dropped the train, which busted into wheels and axles, a smoke stack and a clickety-clacker. "Oh, no," Crusty comforted the sad elfling, who saw his hard work in pieces. "We can fix this in a jiffy," he assured the child. "Let us first hear what's got Santa all grumpy this time."

Everyone in the now-quiet Toy Shoppe heard the comment, including Santa, who patiently waited for the old elf to compose the elfling. Whereas Jackie was always quick to trigger Santa's impatience, Crusty had the opposite effect on Santa. Crusty's age, experience, knowledge, and history always commanded respect and patience from The Pole's leader. Perhaps the only thing Santa would ever argue over with Crusty was, curiously, Jack's idol, Krampus. Like Jack, Crusty felt Krampus was merely a misunderstood monster. But as Crusty would say, "Aren't we all?" Crusty finally stuck an ancient brass hearing trumpet to his ear, which helped him hear about every other word—Crusty just made up the rest to fill in the gaps.

Candi and Jack rushed in nearby, and with all eyes on him, Santa took a long and overly-dramatic moment to read the poster before showing it to the elves. "Christmas uncanceled?!" He looked about the curious, surprised elves, suspiciously pausing on Jack. "Whose bright idea was this?" Everyone looked to one another, but nobody fessed up, believing it was really Santa's idea. "Hear me now," he said. "Christmas is not happening."

Jack stood forward, ignoring Candi's tug at his sleeve to stay back. "It's not yours to cancel, sir."

"Rumpus."

He took another step forward. "We've worked too hard. All year!" Most of the elves looked incredulous at Jack…here we go again. "Mickie," Jack turned a palm out towards his nemesis. "He busted his…jingle bells. Or something." Mickie nodded in agreement.

Santa protested. "My leg is-"

"We have hordes of reindeer," Jack interjected. "And we can all chip in and deliver, so it's not like we can't manage." More elves mumbled their agreement.

"It is dangerous."

Jack pointed to the large *Days To Christmas Eve* calendar next to Santa. "We got time to practice." More elves rallied behind Jack. "But when you think on it," he frowned, "don't the reindeer just fly themselves?"

"The reindeer need," Santa paused, frowning. "No! End of discussion."

"Why? Why's that the end of discussion?"

The elves now cheered, much to Santa's surprise. He looked about…what the hell? He mustered up the bluntest and blank expression he could find to drive a threat home to Jack. "Because I am the boss, Rumpus."

"Kids are counting on you," Jack said, and some elves shouted that they wanted to help.

"Jackie…"

But Jack cut him off, starting to chant, "Un. Can. Cel! Un. Can. Cel!" And the elves all started to join in the chant. Some hopped onto their workstations, waving their mallets and saws and screwdrivers. Santa sighed, realizing he could be facing a revolt.

Crusty, caught up in the excitement, chanted along with what he heard in the hearing trumpet. "Rum. Bar-rels! Rum. Bar-rels!" he laughed at the fun.

"Fine," groaned Santa, pointing his cane at the dying commotion. "But we do this my way."

And then…a roaring cheer as Christmas was once again, although this time officially, uncanceled. Santa stared at Jack, who turned to Candi with an excited whisper. "I'm going to meet Krampus!"

Although Jack whispered right into her ear, that distance Candi felt between them screamed ever so loud. She felt defeated, dejected, and needing to re-think her next steps.

# 3 - REINDEER GAMES

Santa worked at his desk, double-checking his lists for which kids wanted what toys, and trying to figure out how his new plan might work…or even if it could work at all, when he remembered he had forgotten to double-check a specific list. An important list. A missing list. He looked for it under papers. A quick check through drawers. He thought he saw some scraps under his desk and crawled underneath to investigate. The Missus entered at that point, reviewing some reports. "All parties accounted for!" she announced, startling Santa, who gave a frustrated grunt when he bumped his head on the underside of the desk. The Missus looked up from the reports and over her reading glasses. "Dear?"

"I reckon this Christmas is gonna be the end of me," Santa moaned, climbing up and rubbing his head.

"From a bump on the noggin and a broken leg? You've run Christmas Eve with far more complaints than that. Remember the year you had the stomach flu and the Sugarplum Trinkles?" Santa groaned, collapsing into his chair. The Misses paused, trying to read his melancholy. "And you go telling the wee ones I canceled Christmas."

"Had to defer to a higher authority," he smiled.

"Higher authority? Now I know something's troubling you."

Santa pursed his lips together, thinking, and it was in that exact moment when he finally realized why it had been the Year of the Crab, just what had been troubling him, that *something* that he had to do something about. His eyes met hers in a thoughtful embrace until hesitant words finally slipped from him. "I'm old."

"Nonsense," she dismissed him with a nod. "Santa doesn't grow old."

"I know I don't look old." He caught his reflection on the computer monitor. "Well, any more ancient than I should look. But I feel it." He looked into his reflection a moment, mouth slightly agape, and then made a *tck* noise from his cheek. "Yes," he nodded. "Old. That's what I've been feeling."

She dropped the report onto his desk and sat on his lap, wrapping an arm across his back. She nodded to the pages. "Flyers and Helpers. Whenever you're ready to pass the baton, I'm always with you. We'll grow old...er. Together."

Santa leaned into The Missus for a hug. "I haven't anyone to pass the baton to."

"Maybe one of the Flyers?"

He picked up the list and skimmed it, considering the idea. "Lists, lists and now more lists," he said, shaking the report before tossing it back onto his desk. He paused when a specific name caught his attention. "Jackie Rumpus? He's..."

"Mischievous. Not quite unlike a certain elf I fell in love with once upon a time."

"I was never mischievous."

"You were on the Naughty List more often than not. I suspect that's why you and Jackie are always butting heads. Give him a chance."

He sighed in a tone that confessed his love for her. "Did you give me the Naughty List?"

"I did."

Santa shook his head with another sigh; this one with a twinge of frustration. "Mischievous, you say? He must have taken it."

"Jackie?" She hopped off his lap and began searching about. "Why would he steal the Naughty List?"

"I can't fathom." Santa thought, tapping the end of his nose. "Kinda curious what he's up to, now."

Signaling the end of their shift, the current day on the *Days To Christmas Eve* calendar tore itself off and grew large as it drifted over the factory floor, finally dissolving into a brief, yet refreshing snowfall. "Teams of two!" Santa boomed, overlooking the crowded Toy Shoppe floor. He leaned on his cane and pointed about with a scroll. "Flyers and Helpers. Flyers deliver. Helpers remain at Headquarters to guide and track. Your first training will also be your tryout. Some of you won't make the cut. Any questions?" Santa took in the silence that followed with an appreciative side glance at The Missus. The elves remained quiet, for even if they had questions, now wasn't the time to ask them. But, of course, they all shared that one burning question…*Is my name on your list?* Santa unfurled a long scroll while putting on his reading glasses. "Jingle will ride. Partner, Winter." Jingle and Winter hopped about, excited to be called. "Angel rides. Partner, Star Cookie." Angel and Star Cookie shrieked, jumping about, holding hands. Santa realized it would take forever to get through his list if he waited for everyone to calm down when a name was read, so he pushed on through the shrieks, shouts, and hopping as he called out Flyer and Helper teams. "Tinsel and Holly. Sugarplum and Ginger. Sunny and Evergreen. Feliz and Mickie."

"Yes!" Mickie fist-pumped the air, turning to Jack. "In your face!"

But Mickie's gloating wasn't to last long, for the next team announced was "Rumpus and Candi." Jack leaned into Mickie's face with wide, happy eyes. "Oh, yea! Ho…ho…ho…"

"Snowball and Pixie," Santa continued but then was interrupted by Candi.

"Santa? Why am I at HQ?" Jack spun to her, glaring. "I know how to fly."

"Because I need you to keep Jackie out of trouble."

Candi looked about as elves giggled. "Can't I ride instead?"

Santa's cheeks pulled up slightly so that his teeth showed. He shook his head. "I don't trust Jackie to keep you out of trouble." The giggles turned into laughter, and Jack's glaring became even more…glaring.

"Well, why send either of us out at all?"

Santa cocked his head askew, put his hands on his hips and paused. "Why did you sign up if you didn't want to go?"

As she began to answer, Jack's goofy eye threats morphed into a more pleading look. She paused on his wince. "Nevermind, Santa. I'm sorry." Jack was curious but relieved.

Santa returned to his list. "Buddy with Crumpet." Upon hearing her name, Crumpet began squealing so obnoxiously, it gave everyone a start. Before Santa could continue, he was interrupted, yet again. This time, by Jack.

"Santa?"

"Now what!?"

"Can I have Rudolph?"

"What?" Santa scratched his head, annoyed. "No, you can't have Rudolph! Or any of the other eight."

"Well, who gets Rudolph?"

Santa put his hands back on his hips. "No one gets Rudolph!"

Jack shrugged. "So he'll just be staying at The Pole? Doing nothing?"

Santa returned to his list, dismissing Jack by speaking to the paper scroll in front of him. "If I stay home, my team stays home. Call it a vacation this year." He waved his hand to further dismiss Jack.

"Vacation? From what? What have they been doing all year?"

The Santa Look peered from over the top of the scroll. "Can we please just proceed? Noel with Jingles. Sirius with-"

"How about…" Jack's eyes grew wide, his mind already imagining zipping about the globe, his reindeer team led by none other than the one beast Santa didn't trust enough to ride himself. "Noxen?!"

"Noxen?!" The scroll crinkled in a slight grip. "No! He's dangerous and untested."

Candi stepped forward, similar to how she might defend Jack. "He's only untested because you won't give him a chance!"

Santa frowned, staring at her in disbelief, mouth slightly agape, not noticing the smirk and the atta-girl wink The Missus threw at Candi. All sorts of suspicion clouded his mind as he partnered-up Sirius with Swizzle…had Candi been riding Noxen?

The next day, the tryouts came. Outside by the reindeer barn, rows of tiny reindeer waited patiently at their tiny sleighs—bridled, in teams of eight, as excited as the elves who were lined up like rows of military awaiting orders and wearing wireless headsets. Santa walked through the ranks of Flyers.

Feliz nudged Jack on the shoulder. "Don't muck this up, Snowflake!"

Some of the elves giggled, but Jack was too excited and anxious to care. He adjusted a pair of steampunk goggles and dismissed Feliz with his standard "Whatever," as his palmed flipped out.

Inside North Pole Headquarters, rows of elves sat at computer stations, also wearing wireless headsets. Candi's console showed a radar app in one corner—where a white blip indicated Jack and red blips indicated the other elves. A countdown-to-Christmas Eve app ticked away in another corner. Other random computer background noise filled the remainder of the screen—social media, Solitaire, a chat session, and the like. The Missus walked the ranks of Helpers.

"Teams will be sent up in groups of three," she explained. "They will practice takeoff, simulate a near collision, and of course landing." She paused at Mickie's station and waited for him to acknowledge her. He didn't, of course, for he had gotten lost in a game of Mad, Mad Reindeer Madness. The Missus craned her neck as a round of glowing snowballs shot from his avatar's reindeer antlers into a crowd of zombie snowmen. The glowing snowballs sizzled through the enemy horde and made quick puddles of them.

Candi clearing her throat finally snagged Mickie's attention. He jerked his head her way and then Candi nodded up towards The Missus. His gaze slowly followed up to where Candi looked, into the stern and sarcastically-patient woman staring down at him. "Gah!" he jumped, as a sorry squeezed through his grimace. The Missus pursed her lips together and let her silence speak that he needed to take this seriously as she continued down the aisle of workstations.

Outside, Santa instructed the Flyers to check in with Headquarters. "Jack Krumpus, checking in."

"Who?" Candi shot back through the headset.

"Jack. Krumpus."

"Krumpus?"

"Candi…" Jack crouched over his mic, annoyed, as other elves excitedly rushed to their sleighs. "Jackie. Rumpus."

"Oh, Jackie! Yes! Jackie Rumpus, proceed to your sleigh." As he crunched towards his sleigh, Candi chuckled into the mic. "I'm so gonna enjoy being the boss of you."

Jack smiled. "Nobody's the boss of me."

Cleared for takeoff, Angel moved her sleigh forward, feeling the random tug of the reindeer team gradually fall in synch with the momentum. Two other teams raced past her and shot up into the sky. Jack climbed into his sleigh, listening to Santa instructing them through the headset, growing anxious and bored while watching Angel and the others go through their exercises. His right leg bounced in anticipation. The tension all down the line of teams felt like a jack-in-the-box ready to pop, waiting on the next crank of the handle. As Angel's group finally started to land, Candi told Jack he was clear to take off. "What? Yes!"

Inside, Mickie threw a sharp look at Candi. "What are you doing?" he asked. She arched her eyebrows, pretending to not know what he meant. "You just send Jackie up?"

"Psh…no!" she answered with a flip of her wrist. She turned back to her monitor to watch the blips, running her fingers through her hair so that it fell like a drape hiding her from Mickie.

Jack snapped the reins over the backs of his reindeer team. "Woo-hoo!" His sleigh gained speed, approaching the back end of Feliz's sleigh. As Feliz waited to take off, he caught sight of Jack approaching, laughing like a madman. Feliz snapped his team to move out of Jack's way. Now, Jack, thinking that Feliz wasn't going to move, hopped to his feet and pulled his team left. And Feliz, not watching what Jack was doing, also pulled into a left. Collision was still imminent. Ecstatic, Jack pulled right. And, of course, so did Feliz. Surrounding elves started their teams to get out of the way, spreading more chaos to ever more teams. Unclear what was happening, or what should be happening, everyone started taking off, filling the sky with reindeer, and Santa too busy speaking with Angel's group to notice.

Noel shouted over to Swizzle. "Are we just all taking off, now?"

"I guess," Swizzle shrugged. And off they went, two more teams launching. Swizzle passed an elf that was just too intimidated to move, while Noel passed an elf who—no matter how hard he worked—could not get the reindeer to respond to his commands.

As Jack's team nosed in on Feliz's sleigh, Jack laughed and hopped onto the front ledge of his sleigh. He yanked back on the reins, looking like he was trying to stop, but instead called out, "Up, up, and away!"

Inside, Jack's laughter brought the biggest of grins to Candi's face. "Up, up and away?" she asked.

And through the headset, she heard, "What do you want me to say?"

"The correct phrase is *dash away all.*"

"Then dash away! Dash away! Dash away all!" His laughter was followed by a very cowboy-like "Yee-hah!" Candi's laughter quickly faded into a sad sniffle. Jack was going to leave her after all, and he would be happy to do so. And she would be happy for him. *Should* be happy for him. If only she weren't so sad and angry about him.

Jack rode high over the snowy campus, weaving in and out of the reindeer swarm. Some elves laughed. Some gripped the reins in terror. Nobody was as excited or as at ease as Jack. "Candi! This is amazing! I wish you could see The Pole from up here, underneath the Lights!" The Lights, he meant, were the Northern Lights, shimmering about them in eerie greenish hues.

"Doesn't Hollyberry Farms look like fireworks in the moonlight?" Jack leaned over the edge of his sleigh to the greenish-blue and red swath that sparkled in the icy landscape—electric, living, undulating.

"Well, look at that!" he said and then thought a curious thought. "Huh…he says."

And inside, Candi jostled at his *huh…he says*, as if suddenly remembering something and then needing to cover her tracks. "Careful, Jackie!" she blurted. "Not sure if your brain knows how to process happy."

Jack laughed, and climbed higher, zipping through other flyers. He then dipped down and barnstormed the town—shooting through alleyways and streets, just tapping the top of a Kettlekart and dashing through its smoke before pulling high up into the sky.

Over by the reindeer barn, Angel and the other two elves looked past Santa, who droned on and on about the most important thing to remember when landing, especially on a rooftop. He asked if any of them had any questions. Angel slowly raised her hand and then pointed to the sky behind him. "Santa?"

Santa turned to where she pointed, and wide-eyed, he gasped, "What the-?"

Among the Helpers, The Missus stopped at Candi's desk when she caught a glimpse of Candi's radar app. "Rumplemints!" she gasped upon seeing all of the activity. Candi and Mickie twisted up their faces at one another…language. Evergreen announced that all riders were in the air just as Santa shouted into all headsets, "Abort! Abort!"

"Oh!" The Missus huffed, relieved. "You heard the boss. All riders grounded!" The Helpers all complied, ordering their Flyers to land.

"Land?" Jack grumbled, unsure he heard right. "Already?"

Feliz spied Jack and then turned his flight path into a game of Chicken. Only, Jack didn't accept the challenge. He pulled left, yet Feliz matched him. He pulled right, and Feliz followed. Nearly colliding, Jack and Feliz corkscrewed through each other's teams. "See how you like it, Snowflake!"

Through the headset, Candi yelled at Jack, "What are you doing, Jackie?" She watched the red and white blips spin and dance about one another on her monitor and looked up and outside through the window.

Jack shouted, "We've been grounded!" He pulled up on the tail of their twist, and Feliz climbed back to him—and when they met again, they shot straight up, with their reindeer teams nearly feet-to-feet. Jack turned away and Feliz followed, pulling them into a wide arc. Feliz corkscrewed around Jack, forcing him higher and higher, and then he side-swiped Jack's sleigh to keep him from descending.

At the reindeer barn, Santa surveyed all the landing teams and then looked up high in time to catch Jack returning a side-swipe at Feliz. "Rumpus!" he growled.

Candi threw down her headset and ran to the window, as did Mickie. "No, no, no, no, no," she mumbled. This got carried away fast. This was not supposed to happen. This was, well, kind of exciting. Other Helpers crowded around them to watch the dogfight.

Feliz slammed again. "Sick of you, freak!" Jack attempted to pull ahead, but Feliz stayed with him. Finally, Jack bumped his sleigh so hard that Feliz bounced out, shouting as he fell.

Inside, the Helpers let out a collective gasp. Mickie pounded against the glass, "Feliz!"

Jack raced on like some crazy stagecoach driver. "Yee-hah!" But then he saw Feliz's team without their driver. He looked down, spotted Feliz falling, and then dove in a sharp twist. Racing towards Feliz, Jack caught up to him so that Feliz fell next to him. Jack pulled up in a sharp hairpin so that Feliz gently landed into the seat next to him, stunned at the rescue.

"Whoa. Snowflake?"

"It's Jack!" He snapped the reins hard, zipping back up to Feliz's team.

Santa caught the rescue, astonished. "Rumpus!" He knew Jack could fly. He just didn't know he could *fly*. The Missus, absently clutching her blouse near her heart, muttered, "Oi! I really am getting too old for this." The Flyers on the ground and the Helpers inside all cheered, but the spectacle was not over yet!

Jack pulled alongside Feliz's empty sleigh. Feliz stared straight ahead as they approached Gumdrop Mountain through cloud cover. "You gotta land 'em," Jack shouted but got no response. "Feliz! They'll slam into the mountainside!" Feliz shook his head…ain't moving. "Fine!" Jack hopped to his feet, handed the reins over to Feliz and then leaped over to Feliz's sleigh. But, in his hurry to steer away from the mountain, Feliz pulled away too soon and Jack missed. Feliz gasped at seeing Jack's fail and stood to see where Jack had fallen.

Everyone on the ground stood enthralled, wide-eyed and tense. "Jackie!" Candi called and turned to run to help, but The Missus put a reassuring hand on her shoulder. Candi buried her face in her warm embrace. She couldn't watch!

Jack dangled, struggling to pull himself up onto the runner and then up and over the side. He slipped back down. Hanging upside down, he took a look at the mountain coming fast. He pulled himself back up, slid over to the opening, climbed in and plopped into the seat, scrambling for the reins. He pulled the team high, into a loop that corkscrewed out into the opposite direction. "Yee-hah!"

"There's our boy," The Missus laughed, nudging Candi to look as everyone cheered. Well, everyone cheered, except Santa. When Jack finally landed and slowed to a stop, Santa marched up to him.

"Rumpus! I'll see you in my office!"

Jack grimaced, watching Santa stomp away toward Headquarters. "So much for Plan B. C. And D. Ugh."

Flyers and Helpers stood side-by-side next to their workstations. Jack and Candi, however, were missing, having been summoned to Santa's office. "In a moment," The Missus began. "Your computers will display either a Christmas tree or a lump of coal. A tree means you're Flying and Helping. A lump of coal? Well…" She nodded, and the workstations updated. Elves groaned or cheered. Some elves who received a lump of coal were actually quite relieved. Still, other coal-bearers protested that it wasn't their "screw-up" and blamed Jack.

Despite Jack and Candi missing, Candi's workstation showed a tree, but whether they'd remain on the team was what Santa needed to figure out. "Tell me why I should keep you on the team!" he yelled across his desk. "You ruined my training session!"

*Plan B.* Jack kept it in mind, as he weighed his options for a response. *Best behavior.* "Because…" he began. "I gave you…" Santa's frown showed no appreciation for his careful words. "Opportunities!" he snapped, hopping to his feet. "Opportunities to see things…that you didn't know to look for?" Jack arched his eyebrows, forcing a smile.

"And to think I thought you might actually take this seriously. You knocked Feliz out of the sky!"

"In all fairness, he knocked me first. Plus, I caught him! And then I landed his team!" Jack thought. "I was awesome!"

"Santa?" Candi spoke up. "The fault was mi-"

Jack stunned her by rushing to Santa's desk. "No! It was my fault. And I'm sorry. I wasn't paying attention. Pulled the trigger too soon. But I promise you, I am taking this seriously. And I will pay attention Christmas Eve." It wasn't like Jack to simply accept responsibility for something gone wrong…especially when someone else was already willing to do so. Maybe, Candi thought, maybe Jack was growing up after all.

Santa stared at Jack for a moment. "Did you steal the Naughty List?"

"The Naughty List?" Jack feigned surprise. "Psh…no," he dismissed Santa's question with a wave.

And Santa stared some more, unconvinced, frozen in The Santa Look.

And Jack's nervousness turned him to Candi with a shrug…why would I steal the Naughty List? But Candi's hopes for Jack maturing fizzled, and she stared at him with her own version of a shocked Santa Look with her eyes fixed on Jack's fingers, which he had crossed behind his back.

## 4 - PERMA-SWEAR

"The Naughty List?" Candi gasped, shoving the scroll back into Jack's chest.

"Shh…" Jack snapped as she looked skittish about.

"You stole the Naughty List," she repeated matter-of-factly as if it was the only logical thing that could have happened.

"It was an accident," he assured her, but clearly she wasn't assured. "Mostly," he shrugged. "It fell. Into my pocket." He thought. "When I fell off Santa's chair." And then he grimaced. "When I snuck into his office."

"It fell." She rolled her eyes. "Into your pocket." She walked a few paces until a sigh born out of pressure finally escaped. "Why?"

"Think about it. Krampus is going to go after the bad kids." He waved the list at her as his eyes skittered about for anyone who might be watching. "To find him, I just need to follow this." She shook her head with a mix of emotions as he tucked the list back inside his shirt. The way she looked at him just now was the same as how everyone else looked at him. "Don't judge me," he snapped. "You're the one who sabotaged me."

"Won't happen again," she grimaced, pacing ahead as somebody bumped Jack from behind. Jack tumbled forward, knocking over Candi and landing on top of her. "Oopf!"

"Are you okay?" he asked.

"Yeah, just fine," she grunted. "I always throw myself to the ground just to land on my face!" She twisted her neck, eyes furious.

Jack slammed his palms against the floor and lifted himself, turning and charging to what he expected to be Feliz and Mickie. But, when he saw it wasn't them, but instead Nog and Peppermint, each with their hands planted on their hips, Jack tumbled over his own feet and landed on theirs.

Nog's anger permeated her entire being, right down to the ends of her long and kinky scarlet hair. "You ruined my Christmas Eve!" she shouted with a stomp.

"No. I. Didn't!" Jack glared back at Candi so she'd feel the barb, but he didn't expose her guilt. Candi looked at the raging and sullen faces threatening Jack and felt totally consumed by that hidden guilt. She didn't want to ruin anybody's Christmas Eve. She didn't know what to expect when she cleared Jack early for takeoff, but it wasn't all this. And if Jack hadn't handled the chaos as well as he had, he would be just as upset as Nog and Peppermint. Probably more so. "Nog," Jack stood. "I didn't do this. I promise I didn't." Peppermint marched away in a disbelieving huff. Nog stared a few moments longer before following suit. At last alone, Jack turned back to Candi and reached to help her from the floor. A sorry glance reached back at his waiting hand before she accepted his help. "Why would you do that to me?"

"Jackie…" she thought, not quite ready to admit her reasons, yet seeing little choice. "Today was the first time in a long, long while that I saw you happy. And it's nice to see you happy." Her palm rested on his cheek. "You've got a beautiful, sweet, smile. You know that?"

Jack frowned, "Huh?"

"And I thought maybe it was just because you were going to fly for Santa Christmas Eve." She swallowed, a little teary-eyed. "And maybe it is, but only because you're still bent on running away." Jack felt a little hurt, and a bit confused. Confused about the hurt. Why would he feel hurt? And why would Candi not want him to be happy? "Well, fine." Candi's sadness mixed with growing anger. "If that is what will make you happy. Go. Run away." She flipped her hands, shooing him away. "Go live with your imaginary friend."

"Krampus is not-"

"I don't care!" she shouted, clenched fists at her sides, startling him. "Just go." She walked away but then turned back with a pointed finger. "But I'll tell you this, Jackie Rumpus. It will be easier to hate you than it will be to miss you." She paused, starting to cry. "And I don't want to hate you."

Candi…hate him? Candi couldn't hate him. At least, that's what Jack needed to believe. She was probably the only one at The Pole who didn't hate him. And how he hated to see her cry! He crossed his fingers behind his back, putting the other hand up as in a Scout's Honor salute. "I promise to come home."

"Don't!" she snapped, still pointing a finger. "Don't make promises you don't intend to keep."

"Seriously. If I don't meet Krampus, I'll come home. And since you think he's imaginary, that's got to be as good as me coming home." He chuckled. And it was the wrong time to be chuckling.

Candi hit him hard on the shoulder. "I'm not a joke," she said, sullen. Jack finally felt that same confusing distance that had been tugging at Candi, and the frustrated desperation it brought. And not just because she had marched away from him. He uncrossed his fingers.

"Candi, I promise!"

She kept walking. "Uh-huh."

"Candi! I…I…" He looked about as if the words he needed were on the floor somewhere. "I perma-swear!"

And that got her attention. Stopped dead in her tracks. She turned back, surprised and suspicious, for a perma-swear is not to be taken lightly…and she doubted he had either the guts or the genuineness to follow through. But he stood there, eyes pleading, his pinky held out as if for a pinky-swear, desperate and expectant. She returned to him, hooking her pinky with his and dared him with a look…go on. And she waited, watching Jack wince. And she waited some more, with Jack's eyes darting about like some trapped animal searching for an escape. And still she waited, until she finally blurted, "That's what I thought." Disappointed, she turned away, but he threw all of his might into clenching her pinky, wrapping their entwined hands with his free hand.

"No!" he gasped, his pinky gripping hers tighter. "I'm just thinking. Perma-swear. Got to get the words right, right?"

Candi frowned...I suppose.

"I, Jackie Rumpus," he swallowed, "solemnly and permanently swear that if I do not meet Krampus on Christmas Eve, then I will return to The Pole." As he completed his swear, white vapor wisped from their fingertips and swirled about, encasing their hands in ice. The initial, freezing jolt simply gave way to their astonishment. "Well, now what?" he asked.

"I dunno," Candi said, knocking on the ice block. "Never done this before."

After several minutes of shaking, hitting, banging the ice against the wall, and the ice still binding them together, Candi grunted and marched down the hall. Jack struggled to keep up—nearly tripping over himself at times—until she tried to drag him into the restroom marked with candy-striped stockings, pointed green and curled elf shoes, and a skirt.

"I can't go in there!" Jack clung to the wall as if the door was some portal to hell.

"I want this thing off me," she insisted, and then started bouncing a little. "Plus, I have to go. Like, really go." She tugged harder.

"Oh!" Jack's eyes grew wide. "No, no, no, no, no." He shook his head, and just to be sure she got the point, he added a final, "No."

"Ugh!" she groaned. "Fine!" She yanked him into the men's room, marked with a similar sign, but with dark red lederhosen. She dragged him to the sink and put their ice-encased hands under the faucet, her legs bouncing all the while. The running water had no effect, except to make her urge to go, well, more urgent. "What are we going to do?"

Crusty entered and paused on them at the sink, and although they didn't know why, they both felt like children, guilty of having done something they shouldn't have done. "Crusty!" they both gasped.

"Ms. Kane?" Crusty observed, curious, for it was the men's room after all. He scratched at the thin white hair on his head. "And Jack Krumpus?"

Jack twisted up his face. "Krumpus?"

"That is the name on your door, eh?" Crusty noticed the ice and chuckled with excitement. "Ah! Perma-swear. Something important conspiring?"

Candi blurted yes as Jack shouted no—but then he quickly caught her glance and corrected himself. "I mean, yes."

Candi lifted her hands for Crusty to see. "How do we undo this?"

"A perma-swear? Oh, no" he clapped. "A perma-swear can't be undone."

"Not the perma-swear," Jack explained. "The ice."

"Oh! Well, that depends." Crusty's deep, sullen, and yet bright and ancient eyes, darted back and forth between them. "Who made the swear?"

"Me," Jack confessed in a way that felt like…well, a confession. Why did he feel like the ice had exposed a lie?

"Jack, you made a promise to Candi?" Jack nodded. Crusty turned to Candi. "And, Candi, do you accept the terms of the promise?"

"I do," she nodded.

"Well, now," Crusty clapped again as the ice shimmered and melted. He gave a feeble ho-ho-ho in appreciation of the magic. "The deed is done."

And with that, Candi rushed into a stall and slammed the door. "Thank you!" she called.

Crusty looked about and then down to Jack. "I am in the right place, aren't I?"

That night, Jack grew restless as he pondered the meaning behind the perma-swear. He didn't want Candi's feelings hurt, but he so did not belong at The Pole…Krampus being real or not. He got out of bed and walked the dim halls. But it would be okay, he thought. Krampus *is* real. Jack knew he had to be. And Jack had the Naughty List…so he was sure to find his Christmas-demon idol. But, what if he couldn't? You can't undo a perma-swear. Could you? Everything they had ever known about perma-swears said no, he couldn't.

The most famous fable they had ever learned on the matter was the story of *The Needy Elf and the Snowman*, from *Dingle's Dozen*—a collection of Bartholemus Dingle's favorite stories written ages ago that all elflings are made to read during their early school years. Jack couldn't remember the exact words, but he remembered its lesson, which was the point of Dingle's fables. It was about an elf who got lost in a blizzard and walked in circles for what seemed like days. Tired, hungry, and freezing, he felt lucky when he stumbled across a snowman, for certainly whoever built him was nearby. He felt even luckier to find that the snowman was alive and could speak! The elf told the snowman that he needed it to show him its maker, and the snowman agreed, but said it needed help, too. It needed two gold pieces from the elf, who did not have any money on him, but lied and said that he did. He made a perma-swear that if the snowman showed him its maker, he would give it two gold pieces. They walked together for a very long while and along the way, the elf told the snowman that he needed its hat, scarf and gloves—for the elf was cold, and being made of snow, the snowman certainly had no need to keep warm. The snowman gave him what he needed. Later, he told the snowman that he needed its carrot nose, for he was famished, and certainly, a snowman had no need for a carrot nose that he couldn't actually smell with. The snowman gave him what he needed. When night came, the elf said he needed its coal eyes and branch arms, for he needed to make a fire. And, most certainly, a snowman had no need for coal and branches. The snowman again gave him what he needed. Morning came with the sun rising over a small village in the distance. The elf thanked the snowman for his help and darted away.

"But, wait!" called out the snowman. "My gold pieces?"

The elf laughed. "Certainly a snowman has no need for gold!" And as he turned away again towards the village, a cold wind swirled about him and he turned into a snowman, a spitting image of the one he had just swindled! The snowman, however, melted away, revealing an elf in ragged and wet clothes.

"I don't need your gold pieces anymore," said the elf, who pulled a handful of coins from his pocket. "I had money all along, but you see…a snowman certainly has no need for pockets."

The elf-turned-snowman, he looked astonished at his predicament. "But, you said you would show me your maker!"

"Oh, friend," said the snowman-turned-elf, patting him where his shoulder used to be. "I made myself. When a broke a perma-swear." And then the elf laughed and ran to the village to buy himself a hot meal and a comfortable bed for, no longer being a cursed snowman, he most certainly had a need for such things.

"Maybe a perma-swear can't be undone," Jack thought. "But would I turn into a snowman?" He huffed. "Ridiculous." His wanderings led him out from the dorms; past the rec area, where a few elves shot pool and played ping pong; past the gym, where Mickie spotted for a sweaty Feliz, who groaned as if the weight he pushed from his chest was the most impossible weight to lift; past the cafeteria; past the entrance to the Headquarters offices, which looked positively spooky at night all empty and dark. His wanderings finally found him in the postal area—a long hall, empty and dimly lit at this hour, flanked by post office boxes floor to ceiling. Jack went to one of the walls, dug into his pocket and pulled out his key. As he reached for the wall, the boxes began to shift—like one of those picture puzzle grids with just one square missing, and you can move just one square at a time to try and create the picture. Boxes slid left, then a column shifted up, boxes slid right, a column dropped down, over and over again until Jack's box landed square in front of him. His key shot out of his hand and into the lock. He reached in, pulled out a scroll and was startled to see a pair of eyes looking at him from the other side of his P.O. box. "Crumpets!"

The owner of those eyes, smiling under thick white bushes, was the Postal Elf. "Jackie? What are you doing up so late?"

"Can't sleep."

"Out for a walk, then."

Jack nodded. "The darkness finds my way." The eyes frowned…okay. "Why are you working so late?"

"This time of year? Desperate kids writing for this or that. Promising they've been good. Plus…Santa finished your assignments."

"Assignments?" The eyes nodded toward the scroll. "Jack opened the long scroll to find two lists—Naughty and then Nice. "Nice?" he winced, thinking. "Snowballs!" He darted off into the dark, the unfurled scroll trailing behind him like a toilet paper tail.

The eyes darted left and right. "Jackie?"

After a long night, the Postal Elf finally emerged from his office tucked behind the P.O. boxes. But before he could lock the door, a chirping, grinding noise echoed in the far dark. "Hello?" he called, before going to investigate. "Who's there?" As he entered the dark hall, a pair of red, angry eyes began to glow, followed by more chirping and a sinister, mechanical laugh. He jumped back but then relaxed as a toy robot waddled into the dim light. He picked up the toy and gave it a look-over. "Curious." It was curious because it was the kind of retro-toy most kids never asked for any more—the kind of robot that walked and chirped and did little else. It didn't tell the weather. It didn't play games. It didn't even talk. Aside from its glowing eyes, it had a round antenna atop its head that spun as it walked; the kind of scary robot that would scare only movie-goers from the 1950s. It was curious because it was walking the halls alone. Curious, indeed. For Jack used that moment to sneak out of the dark and dart into the post office. He quickly scrambled inside and dove under a sorting table should the Postal Elf come back, and he did, muttering, "Curious."

The lights flickered on, and the Postal Elf walked right over to where Jack crouched, hiding, and set the toy down on the table just over Jack's head. He hummed as he walked over to a computer and typed in a search for "robot, retro" and looking it over once more, he added "50s sci-fi." When the search completed, he read aloud, "Randy Jones." And a moment later, "On the Naughty List? Well, that's that then. Perhaps next year." He scribbled his notes onto a paper scrap, taped it to the robot, and left Jack in the darkness.

Jack waited a few minutes to be sure the Postal Elf wasn't returning, and once sure, he scurried out from under the table, hit the lights, and got busy. From reviewing his own Naughty List, he had decided he was going to spend his Christmas Eve traveling the United States, specifically the Midwest, and even more specifically, the suburbs of Chicago, starting in a specific town called Algonquin. What he needed to do now was find all the other Flyer and Helper assignments where there would be overlap with his plan and steal the Naughty kids from anyone Jack might otherwise cross on Christmas Eve.

Sitting at the work table, next to the toy robot, he started with Jingle and Winter's list, working through the Naughty names and trying to figure out roughly where they would be Christmas Eve. "Oh, this is going to take until Christmas Day next year!" he lamented. At the end of it all, he realized Jingle and Winter must be assigned to Iceland, Greenland, and northern Europe. He sighed, trying to figure out a faster way to get through all the lists, but the toy robot kept distracting him.

Had the Postal Elf thought to look, he would have found *J.R.* under the right foot. Jack's initials. Jack's toy. Not that he was still in the habit of playing with toys; but this particular toy held bittersweet sentimental value. The robot earned him his Electric Toy – Level One Badge for the Elf Brigade. That summer, he and other elves worked with Crusty learning how to progress their toy-making skills beyond the simpler wooden toys, stuffed toys, and otherwise wholesome fun. At the end of the semester, Crusty's students had to build a simple electric toy to earn their badges. Many chose remote-controlled cars and planes. Some chose animated puppies and dolls that could somersault. Hints of Jack's inner darkness came through with his robot project: The Decimator—a retro-futuristic horror that once terrorized kids at the drive-in theaters.

Other elves teased him as he progressed on this final assignment—telling him his robot was "too scary" for kids, and he would never get his badge. But Crusty saw something the other elves didn't. As he reviewed the final projects with the class, Crusty announced, "It's not easy work making dark and scary to feel less-so dark and scary." He set the toy in motion across a tabletop. It waddled, the evil eyes glowed, and it laughed its sinister laugh. "And this toy," he proclaimed, "is not so dark and scary." He chuckled at the hokiness as the antenna atop its head began to spin. Crusty gave Jack the highest marks he could give and handed Jack his badge. Jack had never been so proud. And maybe it was out of jealousy. It could have even been out of fear, for folks tend to fear what is different—whether that difference was a good thing like getting the highest marks possible, or as insignificant as having hints of dark in one's personality—but that was the first time Feliz uttered *freak*. And the class laughed, and suddenly, the way they all looked at Jack felt heavier than a look. And Crusty, seeing Jack's happy moment ruined in an instant, turned Jack aside and spoke so that the other elves couldn't hear. "Bright and happy come easy to most elves, Jackie. But some of us have to work for it. And we don't know why. But once we accept that it's okay to have to work for it, the work is much less…work." And Crusty nodded with a wink, sending Jack on his way to ponder his words, calling out, "Good work, Jackie."

Jack touched the toy, standing lifeless and idle on the Postal Elf's table…how ancient it felt. He rolled up Jingle and Winter's list, stuffed it back into the P.O. box and moved on to Tinsel and Holly. But as he sat back down, and moved the robot out of his way, he had a thought. Randy Jones was on the Naughty List. And the Postal Elf discovered so from the computer. Jack took the list over to the computer and typed in the first name on the list—Elsa Nowak. The computer took a moment and then reported that ten-year-old Elsa, from Olsztyn, Poland, most wanted a new computer for Christmas. But Elsa was also on the Naughty List. Jack wished he knew what Elsa had done to earn her lump of coal this year, but that wasn't what he needed to know. She was from Poland, so he could roll up Tinsel and Holly's scroll and move on to the next.

Sunny and Evergreen covered all of Australia. Snowball and Pixie had parts of Africa. Noel and Jingles, South America, along with Sugarplum and Ginger. A search on Miguel Guerro was Jack's first hit in the United States—Sirius and Fornax. He set aside their scroll to continue on his searches. An hour had passed before another hit—Angel and Star Cookie. By the time he had reached the last scroll to search, he could hear the Kitchen Elves in the cafeteria just arriving for the breakfast shift. He had to hurry. When he searched for the name Amy Doohan, he got the final hit—Feliz and Mickie.

"Ugh," Jack groaned. "Why'd it have to be Feliz?" He grabbed the scissors from the worktable caddy and cut off the Naughty portions of the three lists, stuffing them into his shirt. Then he cut off his and Candi's Nice list and, just as he started cutting it into three parts, he realized that if he cut it into three, he'd have to tape it three times—and using tape is something Jack never could get the hang of. The Wrapping Presents – Level Two Badge forever eluded him. And so Jack decided to give all of his Nice kids to the one elf he liked the least—Feliz.

But if taping a box wrapped in festive paper challenged Jack, trying to tape together two scrolls was darn near impossible! "Rumplemints!" Feliz's scroll would try to roll itself shut just as he lined up his Naughty list to the end and reached for a piece of tape from the dispenser. And then, when he thought he had everything in place just right, he'd manage a long piece of tape that would curl and stick to itself before he could stick it to the scrolls. And then he'd have to unstick it from itself, only to have it tangle around his arm. Then he decided to tape each corner of the scrolls to the worktable, but that only caused the scrolls to snap shut, rolling around one another into a tangled mess. And then, trying to get the tape off from the corners, he tore the paper—requiring even more tape to fix it. By the time he was done—he wore tape like all those Elf Brigade badges he had failed to achieve, and Feliz's scroll was taped haphazardly, and a sticky mess covered the work table.

The smell of pancakes and sausage cooking made his belly grumble, reminding him that the Postal Elf would surely return soon enough. He quickly cleaned the worktable, rolled up Feliz's scroll, and climbed the rolling ladder to put it back into Feliz's post office box. But just as he reached into the box, the wall began to move—someone was getting their mail! And whoever it was could hear the faint cries of Jack, as he sped along with his arm stuck in Feliz's post office box—all the way up, all the way over, back to the right, down a few rows, back to the left a few columns, up, over, and when he went all the way down—legs and free arm flinging about—he slammed against the floor and rolled away as the wall continued to shift.

"Oh," he held himself, curled up into a ball around his arm, which stung from getting P.O. Boxed. But, hearing the keys rattling in the office door, he sprang up, grabbed his toy robot and scroll from the work table and hid, sneaking out behind a tired and weary Postal Elf entering to face another long work day.

The Postal Elf shuffled over to where he had left the Decimator the night before and rubbed his hand over the empty spot that remained…as if maybe he couldn't trust his eyes. He turned about. "Curious."

Jack stumbled into his room and fell fast asleep just as he face-planted onto the bed when a knock at the door roused him. "Oh," he groaned. "Go away."

Candi knocked again. "Jackie?" He grumbled and answered the door with half-open eyes. "What have you been up to?" she asked.

He swayed a moment before answering. "What makes you think I've been up to anything?"

To his surprise, she snapped open the scroll with their assignments, cut in half. "Interestingly-"

Jack felt about his shirt and looked around his room. "How'd you get that?"

"We haven't any Nice kids! And you-" She paused to rip a piece of tape stuck to the side of his face. "Never could get your Wrapping Presents badge."

"I got my Wrapping Presents badge."

"Level *Two*," she nudged.

He stopped, shoulders drooping as he shuffled back towards the bed. "I never wanted that badge."

She followed him in. "You and tape are not friends." She waited for him to confess his actions, but he ignored her. "Jackie, we have to come up with our flight plan today. How will we do that if half our list is missing?"

Finally, he sat up, looked himself over and tore a piece of tape from his vest, sticking it over Candi's mouth. "I'm exhausted. I spent all night going over everyone's assignments and looking for overlap."

She peeled the tape from her mouth. "Overlap."

"I *accidentally* stole the Naughty List, but, turns out…it's all computerized. Santa doled out Naughty and Nice to everyone, so I had to get everyone's lists sorted out. How could I *possibly* get to *all* the Naughty kids in a single night?"

"Santa does it," she shrugged. "Plus the Nice kids."

"I'm not focusing on the Nice kids, Candi. Just the Naughty. And, now, I'm only going to the Great Lakes area. Midwest. For whatever reason there seems to be a higher concentration of Naughty kids in the Chicago suburbs. Candi twisted up her face…that's odd. "So I had to take the Naughty kids away from anyone else assigned to that area."

Her head cocked askew. "What did you do with our Nice kids?"

"I re-assigned them," he shrugged.

Over in the cafeteria, Mickie had just sat down to breakfast when Feliz rushed up with their scroll. Both were excited about getting their assignments. Feliz gave it a snap, and it unfurled to an obnoxiously torn and taped list where the Naughty portion was completely missing, only to have been replaced by another section of Nice. Mickie paused, mid-chew, "What do you suppose happened here?"

# 5 - HAPPY CHRISTMAS EVE!

When the *Days To Christmas Eve* calendar finally tore itself off the last sheet to Christmas Eve, in addition to drizzling snowflakes at the end of the last shift, it shot fireworks over the factory floor. Brilliant, booming, festive, with crazy holiday shapes and animations—like a glowing Santa sleigh charging through a blizzard snowstorm, led by a bright red glow. The elves all cheered and high-fived one another for a job well done. Many would get the Christmas party started early by heading over to Thimble's for rounds of peppermint ale. The true party wouldn't start until Christmas Day night after Santa had returned and had a chance to rest.

With the Helpers and Flyers all chipping in to deliver this year, the pre-tradition tradition got a little muddled. As soon as the cheering died down, Santa appeared on the catwalk, inviting all to a special *Breakfast With Santa.*

Candi slid her tray along the food line in the crowded dining hall, piling her breakfast high—scrambled eggs, pancakes, bacon and sausage…her excitement for the day ahead had her feeling hungry. Not just hungry, but *hungry*…as if a rick of bacon would calm her any. When Mickie pulled in alongside her and greeted her with

"Happy Christmas Eve," she looked at him sideways for only a moment before returning the greeting.

"Happy Christmas Eve, Mickie Rooney," she smiled, keeping her eyes set on the batch of grits being put out.

"Where's your boyfriend?" he chided.

"Where's yours?"

"Oh, burn!" Mickie laughed. "You know what's interesting? Feliz and I have no Naughty kids on our list."

"Really?" Candi frowned. "You don't say."

"I think Jackie mucked things up."

She slid her tray forward, deciding what best to say. Denial? Confess? She had decided that deflecting would be the best course, but then her mouth opened and betrayed her. "What would Jackie want with your list anyway?"

"I never understood what you see in that freak."

Candi slapped her tray, just hard enough to slip he'd pushed a button. It was a small reward for Mickie, though. Everyone knew Jackie Rumpus was an easy button to push on Candi Kane. She turned away from the food, fire in her cheeks, as she readied to push some buttons herself. But she calmed quickly; took a breath. "You know, Mickie Rooney, I don't pretend to understand Jackie. But I know this much. He's a true friend. The truest friend I've ever had. And he's kind. And gentle…" She frowned, and added, as if to herself, "Once you get past the harsh." She nodded her thanks to the Kitchen Elf who handed her a small bowl of grits.

"He's got a good heart. Which is probably more than I can say for what's standing before me." Then she looked up and nodded. "Happy Christmas Eve, Santa."

"Happy Christmas Eve," he returned. Mickie's eyes grew wide as he turned and looked up at Santa's disapproval. But Mickie got off easy, for Santa's look was all he got. Santa frowned and then took his trays from the Kitchen Elf and went to join The Missus at the head table, where they were joined by Crusty and other elders and teachers. Santa was so preoccupied he barely touched his food, staring off into the space of the room, listening to the background noise of ecstatic elves enjoying each other's company.

"Breakfast is about over, Dear," said The Missus, resting her hand on Crusty's arm as she turned back to Santa. Santa said nothing. "Are you going to make your speech?" Still, nothing. "Well, the least you could do is stop ignoring me."

"I'm not ignoring you," he said, sipping on his coffee. "I don't know what to say. I don't wish to scare them."

She patted him on the back and kissed him on the cheek. "Then don't be scary."

He nibbled some toast, thinking Most of the elves hadn't ever been away from the North Pole before. And the world could indeed be a scary place, he worried. He panned the room for Jack, finding him looking a bit preoccupied himself alongside Candi. Finally, Santa sighed, stood up and waited for the din of the room to dissipate. "Good morning, everyone." He cleared his throat. "And Happy Christmas Eve."

"Happy Christmas Eve!" the room shouted back, jolting Santa to a smile.

"This year, we're doing Christmas a bit differently. And I appreciate the enthusiasm and excitement you all have shown. For all your work in the Toy Shoppe this year, I give thanks." He nodded and toasted the room with his coffee mug.

"Hear, hear!" the elves shouted back, clinking their mugs.

"Some of you are going to discover today just how big the world is." His concerned eyes surveyed the room for all his Flyers. "Try to stay out of trouble. It's not just about not being seen. Or avoiding planes. Or being cautious in war zones. You just never know what lurks beyond the chimneys you enter." The rosiness on the elves' cheeks all flushed. Their eyes widened. And, under the table, The Missus kicked Santa's leg. "Oh!" he winced, turning to her with clenched teeth. "My good leg!" She smiled at him as a reminder, with laughter filling the room. He turned back to the elves, pausing in particular on Jack. "Yes, well, what I mean to say is, it's all about the children. Always remember our mission is all about the children."

A few elves picked up on who he spoke to. Feliz leaned over and whispered, "Yeah, Snowflake."

Jack dismissed him with a wave, locking eyes with Santa who continued his speech. Something odd and familiar hit him from those eyes. A darkness maybe? Fear? Worry, for sure. Santa, lately seemed less…Santa-y, and perhaps a bit more like himself. Like, no matter where Santa was, he was always someplace else.

Planning something else? Jack squinted a little, a thought twisting his face...*scheming?*

"First round, check in..." Santa glanced up at a clock. "Three hours. Happy Christmas Eve!"

"Happy Christmas Eve!" the elves shouted. Many stood to take their trays to the tray return and get ready for Flying and Helping, or celebrating at Thimble's.

In the commotion, Jack's thoughts returned to his mission. He leaned into Candi and whispered, "I have to finish packing."

"Okay," she smiled, and her happiness threw him. Like Santa, she was someplace else. A happy place, but scheming something just as well. "Catch up with me before you leave."

He frowned, "But...I'm leaving...now."

"The Pole, I mean." And as he walked away, she chuckled, "Dork."

Later, Candi waited for Jack at the long windows in the corridor to North Pole Headquarters. She rested her forehead against the cold, refreshing glass, watching the latest round of Flyers launch in the far distance by the reindeer barn. The town below bustled with excitement. The crowd overflowed Thimble's and spilled over to the slightly sketchy Nutcracker Tavern. And with each Flyer taking to the air, the crowds shouted "Hooray!" Kettlekarts zipped here and there, with folks rushing to various celebrations about town. And all the while, Candi watched with an infectious smile. She didn't even care that she wouldn't be able to celebrate this year, being a Helper and all.

Jack tapped her attention back inside. "Candi?" He sounded a bit meek, sad, and yet excited. His Santa uniform was standard issue—red with white trim, though the trim was lightly dyed at the ends in shades of purple with black—as if done randomly with markers. Silver diamond studs embossed on the black boots, which matched the black belt—also embossed around his skinny frame to where a shiny skull grimaced for a belt buckle. Instead of the Santa hat, Jack went with his elf hat—the one where the bell no longer jingled, but rattled with devil horns. And over his hat rested his steampunk goggles.

Candi took in her Goth Santa and bit her lower lip to contain her smile. "Has Santa seen you?" Jack frowned, shaking his head. "You should probably keep it that way." The smile escaped her.

"I'm hoping Krampus will like the nod," Jack smiled back, showing her the devil bells, a little awkward. Then he remembered and grew excited. "And if this is too subtle-" He opened his jacket to show her his workshop vest with *Krampus* etched across the back. His smile fell back to an awkward grimace, but Candi's smile beamed.

"Too subtle?" she huffed.

His eyes arched. "Too much?"

"I don't think so." She adjusted the collar on his jacket. "Got your flight plan all figured out?"

He waved the Naughty List at her and paused, caught between his sadness and excitement. "I guess this is goodbye."

"Uh-huh," she smiled.

"I mean," he swallowed. "For real. For good."

"I know."

Jack didn't know what to make of her smile. "I'm running away. Really." Her laughter baffled him. She laughed, of course, because Krampus wasn't real…just a story to scare Naughty kids into behaving for Christmas. Jack's mouth gaped, and his lips quivered as he searched for his words. "I'll miss you," he finally blurted, as if he desperately wanted to not say so, but the words escaped him regardless.

"I'll see you later."

"Candi?" His confusion on her mood tortured him so.

"You can't undo a perma-swear." She shook her head.

"But I'm going to live with Krampus."

She nodded…uh-huh. But then a seriousness took hold of her look, and she paused, a growing anxiousness in her belly before she finally wrapped her arms around Jack and kissed him. It wasn't one of those Hollywood kisses she had fantasized about for a while now—just a simple kiss. A sweet kiss. A kiss that would let Jack know what they had never before said to one another. That she loved him was obvious. That he loved her, she never doubted. But it was never mentioned. Never acted upon aside from their friendship. That kiss was a line she had decided needed to be crossed in a now-or-never moment such as this. And Jack's wide-eyed surprise and smiling huff made her beaming smile all the more bright. "Maybe you can't undo a perma-swear, Jackie. But maybe that will give you a reason to *want* to come home."

Jack remained still, watching her skip away towards North Pole Headquarters. Her smile flashing back towards him was the brightest thing in his field of vision. His heart fluttered, shocked into happy, yet that made the weight of his sadness all the more heavy. Would this be the last time he would see her? Could their friendship ever be the same if he came back home? Could working alongside his idol, Krampus, ever give him as much joy as he felt in that instant? What was it about him that could take such a moment of happiness, and twist him into sadness?

He looked outside to the teams taking off. He looked about The Pole, at all the festive elves cheering on the Flyers. To the Kettlekarts zipping along. To the snowy campus mixed with modern buildings and ancient fantastic cottages.

And a tear fell.

What was so wrong with him? Why didn't he belong here? How could he be so sure he'd belong with Krampus any more or less than he did at The Pole? Why couldn't he just be a happy, festive elf, celebrating with everyone at Nutcracker Tavern? Why couldn't he just be a Nice elf? Or, at least, a good elf?

# 6 - THE TROUBLE WITH BEING SANTA

Racing his sleigh high on a clear night, Jack descended over the moonlit Lake Michigan, in awe of the Chicago city lights. The rails just skimmed the water's surface, leaving scattering rings in his wake. Jack hopped to his feet, taking in all the cars rushing along a snowy Lake Shore Drive.

"Candi!" he exclaimed, entering into the city and looking up at the skyscrapers. "I never imagined the buildings so big! Bigger than Gumdrop Mountain!" He zipped between buildings, headed for the black John Hancock Tower. "Skinnier than Peppermint Falls!" How the moon and lights shimmered across its glass! "And they sparkle! Like Hollyberry Farms " He twisted away over a rattling el train, and followed along its path. "And trains fly through the city!"

"Jackie," Candi called through the headset, but in his excitement, he couldn't hear her.

Cars bustled along in every direction, heading into the city and out towards the suburbs in twisting, winding roads of golden light. "And cars everywhere."

"Jackie."

He took off his hat and scratched his head, enjoying the cold rush of wind through his black mop. "But if everyone is expecting Santa, why aren't they all snuggled in their beds?"

"JACK!" Candi shouted.

"Gah!" He recoiled from his earpiece. "What?"

"Don't forget you're on a mission."

"Right!" He pulled the Naughty List from the Santa sack. "First up…Randy. Randy Jones, you've been naughty. What's this?"

Right then, Jack spied a young woman, frazzled and exhausted from dealing with the hustle and bustle of last minute Christmas shoppers at her retail job on Michigan Avenue. "I'm sorry!" the woman repeated into her phone, looking both ways and darting between traffic as she crossed the street. "The boss wouldn't let me leave! I didn't even have time to pick up any gifts." That was partly a lie. She glanced down at the bag carrying the one, dismal, random toy she could find for her son, disappointed at how she had let the time get away from her these past few weeks. "Maybe I can find something he'll actually like in the after-Christmas sales." She marched on down towards the train stations, exhaustion and frustration pulling at her face. "Yes, I know you have plans tonight. Call his aunt. She'll get him. I'm maybe another hour." Just then, a cold wind rushed down the street and swirled about her—kicking up drifting snow, spinning up and about her from the ground. "Whoa!" She twisted about in surprise as the whirlwind passed by and the sparkling snow re-settled.

She absently shook her shopping bag, noticing how it suddenly felt some heft to it, now that it had mysteriously been filled with a few gifts her boy would love. She looked about for an explanation for this small Christmas miracle, but saw nothing, not even Jack's sleigh climbing back high into the sky. "I've got to go," she said absently into her phone. "I'll call my sister as soon as I'm on the train."

Jack smiled at the woman's confusion as he pulled back on the reins. He didn't know if her boy was on the Naughty List or the Nice List. He only saw a frazzled mom, trying to calm a babysitter, as she rushed home from work, late on Christmas Eve. She would never know who gave her the toys for her son. Nor would she understand that the gifts were really for her. Her confused relief that her little Christmas had mysteriously been saved sparked the most joy in Jack's heart that stretched an almost mad-like, uncontainable grin across his face. Being Santa, he thought. He could get used to this.

His reindeer team pulled the sleigh high into an arc, flying out of the city and rushing towards a much, much quieter suburb that lacked tall buildings and flying trains. But what this town did have was an abundance of holiday spirit. Evergreens were lit up into giant Christmas trees, oak trunks wrapped in blinking mats of light, balls of red and white light dangled from branches, bushes twinkled in every color. Huge blown up Santas waved in the wind, along with Frostys and snow globes. And as Jack descended upon one such festive street, there were plastic candy canes, mangers with plastic glowing Jesus babies, and an army of nutcracker soldiers. One neighbor, apparently in protest, scattered among his yard bright, silver *Festivus* poles.

"Over there!" Jack pointed to Randy's house on the corner, groaning while taking in all the spirited decorating. "Ugh. It's like the Ghost of Christmas Present puked up all over the place."

Candi chuckled. "What?"

"Tacky, Candi…just…tacky." He stood on the seat, leaning over the edge of the sleigh as some white wooden statues of reindeer had grabbed his attention. Some local teens posed them into rather lewd positions, very un-Christmasy, yet making merry just the same. By the time he looked forward again, his reindeer had already begun swirling into the chimney top, like water down a funnel. "Whoa!" he shouted, but it was too late.

Inside Randy's living room was a perfect picture setting for a holiday commercial—stockings hung at the fireplace, a decorated tree in the corner—broad and festive—Christmas-themed knickknacks throughout. You might half expect a crowd of carolers to waltz in, singing about all the wonderful sales they snagged at the local store. But all there was was a grey and black striped cat, who purred and stretched in his sleep. And aside from that, silence that was about to-

POOF!

Red and green flashes of light sparked from the fireplace, where eight tiny reindeer and Jack's sleigh shot out and crashed into the room. The room lost. Horribly. Furniture, knickknacks, and the tree all threw in different directions…waking the cat who screeched, launched like a rocket and landed somewhere in the mess of the tree.

"Ah!" Jack inhaled, eyes darting about. His reindeer waited patiently in their neat little rows. "Huh…he says." One-by-one, three ornaments fell and bounced off Jack's head. His "oh…oh…oh" gave way to a "Yeow!" when the star tumbled down the branches, and poked him in the head.

"Jackie?" Candi called. "You okay, Jackie?"

Jack licked his lips, unsure of what all just happened. "Did you know reindeer can go down the chimney?"

"What did you do?" At North Pole Headquarters, Candi launched an app on her workstation that showed Randy's house from overhead in a thermal heat image. Her eyes shot wide, seeing the reindeer inside the living room. In other rooms, she could see the sleeping kid and his parents…stirring awake. Her breath faltered watching, until after rolling over, tossing and turning, the family all fell back to sleep.

"I wasn't paying attention!" Jack said. "What do I do?"

"Send them back up!"

Jack lightly tapped the reins over their backs. "Uh…dash away all?" The reindeer slowly turned to him with a look that clearly asked Jack if he was nuts. Jack nearly threw off his wireless headset when Candi's suggestion came through that she go and get Santa. "No! Don't get Santa! I promised him I would pay attention."

"You *weren't* paying attention."

"Exactly my problem! Do. Not. Get. Santa!" He huffed. "I know! Kringle it!"

"Kringle it?" Candi opened a web browser. "What am I supposed to kringle—reindeer removal?" Mickie turned to her with a curious look, but she was too busy to deal with him. A search engine page opened up on her browser to *Kringle*—where the software developers were clearly from The Pole. She typed in *reindeer removal* and scanned the results. "Removing reindeer poop from boots… reindeer from roofs…reindeer stew? Ah!" She clicked a link. "Removing Rein-," she gasped.

"What?!"

"Oh!" she tapped her forehead, eyes clenched. "Unsee! Unsee! Unsee! That's disgusting. Let's just assume you're the first one ever to land reindeer inside a house."

"Woo-hoo!" came back through the headset.

Candi's eyes narrowed. "Focus, Jackie!"

Inside Randy's living room, Jack unharnessed his reindeer team. "No, that's 'woo-hoo,' I got it! I can't get them back up through the chimney, but I can get them through the front door!"

"They won't fit."

"Two-by-two they won't."

Just as he unharnessed the last of his team, the cat launched from the tree and pounced onto the rump of a reindeer—which then brayed and bucked and stirred all of the other reindeer into a frenzy. They flew. They bounced. They jumped and crashed.

Christmas destroyed the room.

Watching, horrified, as thermal images of the reindeer scattered about, Candi's eyes darted about the app. "Oh, oh, oh!" She covered the app with her hand, winced at Mickie, and then when she peeked under her hand she gasped, "Jackie!" for the ten-year-old Randy finally woke, hearing Jack's commotion from the living room…but Jack was too preoccupied to hear.

Randy yawned and stretched, rolling over, entangled in the blankets of his spaceship bed. His entire room was decorated like a scene from a sci-fi movie. His desk and chair were as if a console from the starship Enterprise. His dresser was shaped like a droid, which even lit up and made sounds when its drawers opened. The orange carpet was dotted like some alien terrain, with rock-looking pillows scattered about. The shelves held his prized collection—dozens of his favorite robots—evil and good—from the various galaxies from his favorite movies. Randy sprang up in bed, "Santa!"

Not realizing he had earned a spot on the Naughty List this year, Randy was sure this was the year Santa would bring him the Decimator Robot from the 1950s drive-in creature feature *Martian Mutants*. If he got Decimator, he would be happy. Well, his happiness would last at least a week, maybe even two! But then he would really need to get Decimator's robo-sidekick Golan Brink. And then, of course, all of Randy's happiness would depend on him getting that one…last…next…robot. He had to make sure Santa got it right this year; for he asked for the Decimator last year, but received only an original edition droid action figure from a recent flick—still in the package— autographed by the actor who played him in the film.

Randy crawled out of bed and cautiously stumbled down the hall, to where Jack's commotion grew louder. Crashes. Banging. Shattering glass. And then Jack's shout, "Stampede!"

Candi's voice snapped in the headphones. "You've got a kid on your six!"

"My what?"

"Your six. Behind you!"

Jack turned just as a stunned and awed Randy stepped into the room. A reindeer galloped through the air, rounding the corners of the room and briefly paused face-to-face with the child as Jack bounded across the room. "Randy Jones, you've-"

And with that, Randy fainted.

"Snowballs!" Jack shouted. "I didn't get to say my line."

"You've got eight reindeer swarming." On the Kringle page before Candi, a banner animation began. "Don't worry about the line." A pixelated Santa Claus lumbered across the banner, putting presents under the tree. Candi's eyes widened with an idea. "Your sack!"

"What about my sack?"

"Put the reindeer in it!"

Jack snatched the Santa sack from the sleigh. "Brilliant!" He jumped high from the sleigh and latched on to a reindeer's antlers. Pulling the sack over its head, the beast disappeared inside. "Seven to go!"

Just as Candi muttered "Parents on your-" Jack got startled by Randy's dad, who stood at the start of the hall with the mom.

"What the-" The dad surveyed the completely totaled room—furniture and all—amidst swarming reindeer and their child passed out at their feet.

"Ten," Candi continued. Jack could practically hear her head collapse against the desktop.

Jack jumped, palms outward, and pleaded, "Oh would you please just go back to sleep?" And, much to Jack's surprise, a sloshy, glowing snowball shot from each of his palms, smacking the parents dead center on their foreheads in a sparkling, wet blast. They immediately fell to the ground, fast asleep. Astonished, Jack looked at his palms. "Whoa! Candi…did you know we have superpowers outside of The Pole?"

"What?"

Jack had an idea. He turned his palms out onto the mess of a living room. "Undo." And when everything failed to undo, he snapped "Snowballs!" But then, another idea popped. He shot a glowing snowball at one of his swarming reindeer. The one he hit immediately fell asleep, legs outstretched, blissfully and gently tumbling through the air. Jack laughed and began putting them all asleep, hopping across the furniture, throwing glowing snowballs. "Sleep! Sleep! Sleep!" But one excited reindeer dodged a sleep-ball, leaping over Jack, and disappearing down the dark hallway. "Oh, crumpets!"

A few more sleep-balls quieted the living room. Some reindeer had collapsed to the floor, others floated, gently bouncing off each other and against the walls like fuzzy antlered balloons. Jack looked about the room and sighed. "Candi? I lost a reindeer."

Candi scrolled through the thermal app display to see antlers knocking over shelves in Randy's room. "Down the hall. First door on your left."

Jack cautiously stepped into the dark, hearing a noise from behind the first door on his right. "Ollie ollie reindeer, out in free," he called. And as he opened the door, Candi shouted that she said left, not right. A large, blubbering, St. Bernard charged out. Jack screamed, running and stumbling back into the living room. Jack shot a sleep-ball, and the dog collapsed. Momentum dumped him right on top of Jack, who struggled to catch his breath under the weight of the dog.

"Jackie?" Candi asked. "You okay?" But the only response he had was his heavy breathing. "Jackie?"

The heavy breaths stopped, for he clamped his mouth shut, struggling to avoid the drool that dripped over his face. He pushed with hands. Pushed with his legs and as he finally crawled out from underneath the beast, he lamented, "Lamest. Superpower. Ever." He thought his struggles were over, but then the cat leapt out from behind the couch, attacking the devil-bell on Jack's hat. Jack shrieked and spun about, knocking against the wall. "Aw, c'mon!" Finally, he yanked off the hat and flung the cat across the room. Completely disheveled, Jack huffed and puffed and grunted. "Santa can take his job and-"

At North Pole Headquarters, Santa stepped up behind Candi, startling her when he asked, "Everything okay here, Candi?" But, of course, nothing was okay. Jack's meltdown sounded from the headset, telling Santa he could take his job and shove it.

"Rumplemints!" Candi jumped, tightening her shoulders and back. She ripped the headset off and covered the earpiece, wincing as Santa admonished her.

"Language." Santa leaned in and looked at her monitor as she scrambled to close the heat-imaging app. "Jackie having a problem?"

"Everything is under control sir. I mean!" She straightened, turning up to him. "We're fine!"

"How many deliveries so far?"

"Uh," she swallowed. "One." Mickie sniggered. "We're still on the first," she said, squinting at how bad that sounded to admit.

"Have him pick up the pace. We've only got tonight."

"Yes, sir." She watched him continue walking down the line, occasionally pausing at other workstations, glancing up at the clock. "Santa says to get a move on."

With no sign left of any rogue reindeer in Randy's living room, Jack heaved the heaviest sigh. "I'm done. I'm done." Over his shoulder the threw the Santa sack, which simply looked as if it were filled with toys—not lumps of coal, or all of Jack's belongings, or a sleigh, or eight tiny reindeer. "Leaving now."

"Did you find the missing reindeer?" Candi asked.

"Yes!"

"Did you remember to put a piece of coal in Randy's stocking?"

Jack opened the door to a cool wind that gusted in on the Christmas disaster—a smashed couch, smashed tables, shattered knickknacks, a broken tree, Randy and his parents collapsed on the floor. Jack's eyes surveyed the mess; his heart twinged with guilt. He'd have to remember to stick the landing better at the next house. "Let's just say, uh, yeah." He stepped outside and shut the door, but then had the thought that Randy would never know that "Santa" had visited him if he didn't leave a present, or in this case, that lump of coal. How would Randy know he needed to get off the Naughty List? Or, what if he knew he was on the Naughty List and took the destroyed room for his lump of coal? That would be awful; to think you were *that* Naughty that Santa would trash your living room, yet could not even be bothered to leave a lump of coal. He opened the door again and tossed in a coal chunk, quickly slamming the door shut.

The lump of coal tumbled through the mess, as if it tumbled on its own power. The cat watched it hop over the sleeping dog, roll through the shattered picture frames, rebound against the splintered table leg, and finally rest in front of the fireplace. After a brief moment, a lone spark shot out from the fireplace ashes, and was shortly followed by more popcorn-like flashes, which sparked a flame. A fire roared to life. A shimmering portal opened inside the flames. The cat blinked; turned its head askew. Beyond that portal was a hidden world of fire and brimstone; a seemingly endless pit of rock, with flying reingoyles—reindeer with demented gargoyle heads and bat-like wings.

The hairy shadow of Krampus stepped out of the fireplace, with its long horns, goat legs, slithering tail. As it scouted the mess of a room, its long tongue winded out of its mouth and then retreated. The cat screeched, puffed itself up with a hiss, and then fled—bounding over Randy's face to the safety of a bedroom. The sniveling shadow stepped over to the window. Its large, claw-like fingers pulled back the drapes to see Jack tugging reindeer from his sack and reassembling his team. A sinister chuckle slipped loose.

Randy groaned awake, calling Krampus' attention. The shadow took long steps to him, crunching over broken glass as Randy opened his eyes. "Wha-?" He looked the figure before him head-to-toe. "What the hell are you?"

A basket was thrown at him. Randy shrieked. And Krampus' deep, sinister voice boomed, "Randy Jones, you've been naughty." *Naughty* trailed off into a throaty chuckle. Like a Santa sack, Krampus' basket had a similar magic. Though it didn't have a seemingly endless interior, it held much more space than seemingly possible. A dark space. Cramped when filled with children, for Krampus didn't want to give the Naughty children any semblance of any comfort. Thin beams of light poked in from between the basket slats, landing on the crying children who cowered in darkness and stretched and pulled and fought their way with one another towards those slats so as to glimpse the world outside. Randy kicked and screamed, pushed himself over the other children and reached out from under the lid—only to have it slammed shut on his fingers and hand. Through the slats, he saw Krampus step into the fire, and fearing he would be burned alive, Randy howled.

But Randy's fate wouldn't end him there, for quickly burning children alive wouldn't serve Krampus' mission. As soon as Krampus' long tail slithered through the flaming portal, the portal shut, and the fire dwindled and died.

Outside, Jack launched his team to get back onto *his* mission, not realizing of course, he nearly just accomplished it with Krampus coming into Randy's house just behind him. "Dash away all!" he shouted, as the reindeer climbed into the night.

A fleeting moment of peace weighed heavy upon Randy's living room.

And then, gentle, chilly white wisps of wind blew in down from the chimney and swirled through the room, which magically began to fix itself. Shattered knickknacks unshattered themselves. The fallen tree unfell, and the ornaments hung themselves where they belonged. The star tumbled upwards, bounding over ornaments and lights, righting itself upon the treetop. Splintered furniture pulled together and sturdied themselves. All things unbroken and unfallen. The wisps swirled past Randy's parents, and they lifted, hovering deadlike back towards their bed. And once they were safely tucked away for the night, the wind reversed itself and whooshed back up the chimney.

Finally, Randy's coal bounced up from the floor, landing in his stocking. And, finally, so it seemed, Christmas gasped a sigh of relief for the havoc it righted in the home of Randy Jones.

# 7 - LAME!

After narrowly missing Krampus on his very first stop, Jack fell into a rhythm of zipping along from house to house at a proper elf pace. Candi watched the white dot representing Jack on her radar app blip about her monitor screen as she casually snacked on Polar Bearies—chocolate-covered hollyberry raisins. She had grown bored, and rested her head in one of her palms, watching that dot blip about….until quite suddenly, the blipping stopped.

"What's the matter, Jackie? Looks like you've slowed down."

In the living room of Jeremy Donner, Jack took off his elf hat and scratched his head, for he too, was growing bored. Restless. Half-heartedly, he tossed a lump of coal into a stocking and sighed, "Jeremy Donner, you've been naughty." He looked about the room, expecting his idol to materialize, and began to wonder how Krampus got about on Christmas Eve. Did he have a sleigh? Did he come down the chimney like Santa? For that matter, where was this world he dragged the Naughty kids to? None of these questions were new to Jack. He had even asked Santa about all his curious thoughts. But Santa would never discuss it, telling Jack he should worry less on Krampus and more on the toys he should have been making.

"Still no Krampus," Jack lamented, shooting up the chimney.

"Duh," Candi said, slurping on a Frosted Moon. Though she was speaking to herself, it irked Jack when she added the sing-song commentary, "He's not real."

But Jack, of course, knew Krampus was real. What he realized, though, was that his plan to meet Krampus was not working. "Can you find out why Jeremy Donner is on the Naughty List?" As he took off high into the sky, Jack scrolled through the Naughty List. He could hear Candi navigate her computer, clicking at keys.

"No-go," she finally answered. "I found the file, but it's password protected." Another long slurp. "You want me to try and hack in?"

"No," he sighed.

"Why do you want to know what Jeremy's done?" She listened to the silence of Jack staring into the Naughty List, lost in his thoughts. "Jackie?"

Suddenly, excitement gripped hold of Jack. He hopped up on the seat, thrilled with his own brilliance. Five children, all living in the same cul-de-sac, all on the Naughty List. "Emily, Kevin, Stephen, Ashanti, and Micha...you've all been naughty." As he shot away towards their homes he laughed, "What did you all do?"

Save for Micah, the five children of the cul-de-sac weren't all snuggled in their beds, asleep. Certainly, none of them were waiting for Santa. That would be a lame thing to be doing, after all. Instead, three of them played an online video game about a girl named Alice and her misadventures down some trippy rabbit hole. The Goth kids all talked strategy into their headsets as to how to defeat the monsters with weird little digital weapons they had scrounged while exploring their imaginary Wonderland. Truly mad hats and solving macabre riddles suited them just fine this Christmas Eve as they remained blissfully unaware that, if they weren't careful, similar fates down some different kind of trippy rabbit hole awaited them.

And the fifth child? That would be Ashanti. Less Goth than her former cohorts these days, Ash—as she preferred to be called—held onto only a few reminders of their old friendship. A skull pendant dangled from her bracelet, occasionally clacking against her desktop. Purple eyeliner and matching lipstick that made her dark lips that much darker were about all she cared for for maintaining the look. She even stopped coloring and straightening her hair, and let its natural kinkiness return to its thick, black poof that she sometimes liked to tie into two smaller puffs on the sides of her head.

She knew her fate tonight. Or, at least, she thought she did. She had prepped for it all year long. Like Jack's room, her bedroom paid homage to the Christmas demon. Not with posters, but with books about Krampus and other holiday monsters—countless dog-eared pages, drawings and even vintage Christmas cards she had strewn across her dresser and then spilt onto the floor. She had never heard of him before the year prior, but the more she had thought on it, the more sure she became of one discomforting thing—that Krampus had heard of her. If she was right, the demon had taken a friend of hers, missing since last Christmas Eve, and Ash aimed to get her back.

Unlike Jack, she didn't idolize Krampus. Vague glimpses of him towering over her had crept through her dreams; glimpses that stalked her like a prowling panther. She knew the glimpses were real. They felt real, anyway, yet remained murky enough to maybe be little more than some figment lurking through the tangled jungle of her restless mind. But just in case, she researched and prepared all year long should that figment show its ugly head this Christmas Eve.

Ash had icy blue eyes; an anomaly, she would say, especially given her dark skin. They blinked large and buggy through her steampunk goggles that she had modified with rather powerful magnifying glasses. She peered into the details of a motherboard she frantically tried to solder a wire to. She blew at the puff of smoke. "Should have started with the homing signal," she lamented, before leaning in further to make sure the wire was secure.

Mhambi, one of her inventions, clicked across her desk and tapped one of its spider legs at the motherboard. Its spherical body, slightly larger than a grown man's hand, was made with clear resin so that Ash could peer inside and monitor its computer and mechanical workings whenever she added and tested new features—which would *not* include the new homing signal Ash tinkered with. The idea came to her just recently, having spent much of the year adding the spider legs and drone capabilities. Prior to that, Mhambi was merely a robot ball that rolled about. "I'm not done," Ash shooed away the spider, but Mhambi protested with chitters and more tappings from its front legs. And when Ash further dismissed it with a grunt and a gentle flick from the backside of her hand, the spider added chirps and flickering red light to its argument. "Mhambi?!" she groaned, leaning back in her chair to check the clock on her nightstand. "Seems a bit early. Or late. I dunno." More whistles in protest.

Ash sighed and snatched the plug for the soldering iron from the wall. "A whole year to get ready," she admonished herself yet again. She grabbed Mhambi from her desktop as its legs retreated into a ball shape. Over her shoulder, she threw the strap of her backpack that she had stuffed full of supplies and other gadgets of her own invention…anything she had thought of that might help her on her mission. Anything except the homing device, that is. She snaked her arm through the other strap just in time, as the robot was right—her adventure was just about to start.

While Jack perched his sleigh on Kevin Mahoney's rooftop, Candi's voice sounded in his headset. "What are you up to, Jackie?"

"Think of it, Candi!" In his excitement, Jack's thoughts were so clear that perhaps he wasn't thinking clearly at all. "If Krampus is moving around, and I'm moving around, then he's a moving target." He grabbed his sack and then quickly leaped from rooftop to rooftop across the cul-de-sac, disappearing down each chimney before finally stopping in Kevin's basement. "But if I stay still," Jack explained, "*Krampus* will find *me*!"

"And what makes you think *Krampus* hasn't already paid this kid a visit?" Candi asked her question in such a way that Jack could hear the air quotes, cynicism, and sing-song jab.

But Jack paid her no mind. He shook out his Santa sack, dumping five Goth kids tied to chairs. "Because they're still here." They were all aged between thirteen and sixteen years old. Sobbing Micha was the youngest, and had a black mop atop his head like Jack. Kevin, the oldest, had piercing eyes that threw angry glances about the room. Emily and Stephen were caught somewhere between the two—moody teens, more fascinated than angry or scared. They all wore makeup, though in different amounts and ways so that they could all be unique while still all being the same—black eyeliner; black lipstick; pierced noses, lips, eyebrows and ears; pale makeup; colorful hair—black, white, purple, dark red, blue—Emily had a mix of colors, and clothes fit for a casual Halloween party. Micha, alone, wore pajamas…and the embarrassment alone was enough to make his eternal sadness even sadder.

Ash, of course, didn't wear pajamas…she had dressed for her adventure with her backpack, hiking boots, a cargo vest and shorts whose pockets were stuffed with snacks and gadgets for whatever challenges might come her way. Her magnifying glass goggles perched on her forehead, and the band stretched down and around her poof of kinky black hair. She, alone, was not surprised, for she had prepared for and expected this moment. This moment, however, was not at all what she had been expecting.

"You're not Santa!" Emily snapped, just as Ash casually observed, "You're not Krampus." Emily's many colors, fading softly from one dark shade to the next, much like her thoughts, whipped about as she snapped her motley head. A fluid melancholy. Dark blue blended into deep red, then purple and blackness at the ends. "Who are you?"

"I'm nobody," Jack answered. "Who are you?"

"Emily Dickinson."

Jack frowned. "You're Emily Dickinson?"

"You just quoted her." Her eyes rolled…*duh*.

"I didn't quote anybody." Jack quickly grew agitated. "You're all on the Naughty List."

"What?!" She whipped about towards Kevin. "You said no one would know."

Kevin's angry eyes shot between the kids. "Who squealed!?"

Mhambi slipped from Ash's grip and rolled to Jack's feet. Four legs remained retracted while the other four jutted straight out. Tiny propellers at the ends whirred and spun, and the spider rose, hovering at Jack's face. Jack's eyes widened, curious and fascinated. "Huh…he says." Just then, purplish sparks zapped from Mhambi and shot all around his head. "Gah!!!" he shouted. He dropped a fist on the spider, which crashed to the floor, and he threatened it with a kick before it quickly crawled away and hopped into Ash's lap.

"I don't think she likes you," Ash said, as a tiny spinning serrated blade replaced one of the propellers.

"What is that?" Jack snapped.

"My friend." Mhambi edged closer toward the rope that tied her to the chair.

Kevin jabbed, "Her only friend. Loser." To which Ash glared a threat.

"Shut up!" Jack shouted, taking off his elf hat and scratching the sides of his head. "Shut up, shut up, shut up!" He grunted. "Krampus is supposed to drag you all to Hell. I want to know why."

Micha whimpered. "Krampus? What's Krampus?"

"It's okay, Mhambi," Ash whispered. The spinning blade retreated. Ash nodded back, motioning for the spider to retreat to the backpack. Jack may not have been what Ash was preparing for all year, but Krampus certainly was…and if Jack knew she was on Krampus' Naughty list, she would sit tight and wait for the demon to show.

Emily sighed, growing sullen. "Hell is empty. All the devils are here."

The others all nodded in agreement. Stephen grew a half-smile, just about as much of a smile as was allowed. "Shakespeare. The dark bard. Very cool."

Jack's eyes grew wide. Having to deal with five different versions of himself was proving to be quite the handful. "Quiet!"

"Was it the lame block party?" Emily asked. "I'll bet it was the lame block party. Freaking poseurs."

Kevin snapped at her, "Can it!" Jack noticed how quickly Emily retreated. As Micha whimpered, Kevin turned his rage on him. "Don't be such an emo."

"I'm not emo," Micha sniffled. "I don't even believe in Santa Claus!"

Jack gasped. "You don't believe in Santa!?"

"I'm Jewish!" Micha cried, and although that should have been enough explanation, the meaning was missed on Jack.

Stephen bobbed his head for air quotes, seeing as how his hands were tied. "Thought you didn't believe in *organized* religion."

"Conformist," Kevin shot, and with that Jack hopped onto Kevin's lap, looking thoughtfully at him face-to-face.

"You're the boss here, huh? Everyone's afraid of you?" Jack didn't catch Ash's *as-if* smirk as he hopped back down.

"Let me go!" Kevin shook against the rope. "I'll scream for my folks!"

Stephen laughed, and then in his most dramatic, dark tone, added, "A scream. From the abyss of doom. For Mommy and Daddy!" And then his laughter infected Emily, who laughed to tears.

"Scream all you want," Jack said. "Mommy and Daddy are already…asleep." His fingers ticked as he contemplated more sleep-balls.

"Can it, you!" Kevin snapped, and again, Jack noticed how quickly the others responded to his threats.

"Why do you get to make all the rules?" Jack asked, but he didn't wait for an answer. A sleep-ball flashed, knocking Kevin squarely on the forehead, splattering outward like wet sparks. He nodded back, and then the momentum tipped him just enough so that the chair legs slipped out from underneath. Out cold, on his back. The other kids gasped.

Micha sniffed. "You…you killed him!"

"Fascinating," Emily gaped. "Ultimate freedom."

Jack protested as the kids continued to comment their dark, deathly blackness. Ash quietly contemplated her plans…she had prepared for just about anything, but certainly not this. The other Goth kids couldn't make up their minds on whether they were fascinated or horrified that Kevin was dead. As their bleak-addled banter continued, Ash remained quiet, rolling her eyes with such disdain for their antics that it was a relief when Jack finally could stand it no longer. "Gah!" he snapped. "No wonder Santa hates me! Yes, I killed Kevin. Now shut up and tell me about the lame block party before I get really angry!" The teens summarily all rolled their eyes…as-if. But then Jack raised his hand as a glowing sleep-ball *shlooped* out of thin air and melted into the space below. The threat of their own sleep-ball death got their attention. Ash merely frowned at the threat—for her, every problem had a technical solution; but this, this truly seemed like magic.

"It was all Kevin's idea!" Emily blurted, jerking her head to get her long hair from her face. "Our parents made us go to the party. Which was lame."

Stephen explained that their parents all act like best friends, but really can't stand one another.

Emily sighed, "Poseurs. At least our hate is honest."

Ash shook her head subtly, yet not so subtly pointing out how stupid she thought they all were. Jack stomped his foot and pleaded, "Can we please just get on with it?"

Silence befell the Goth-kids, as their purple and black-rimmed eyes all darted at one another. Finally, Micha blurted out, "We spiked the desserts with diarrhea medicine!"

Emily's shoulders heaved in sudden sorrow. "And then we locked all the little ones inside the bouncy castle." She spoke to the emptiness in front of her. "And before everyone all started getting sick, we locked the porta-potties."

Stephen shed a tear, which left a black trail dripping through the pale makeup on his cheek. "Mrs. Hall yanked on the door. Over and over. And then ran back home. One hand on her mouth; the other on her butt."

"She didn't make it home!" Micha sobbed, shaking his head. "She didn't make it."

Stephen gasped, a memory gripping his throat. "But the kids in the bouncy castle!" The others all looked at him, saddened. "They were still bouncing when it all hit. They tried getting out through the fake windows but ended up deflating the castle."

Micha shook his head. "They had to be peeled out."

Emily stared into the floor as if the mess of her memories had spilt there, anxiously ready to be mopped away clean. "Some people got lucky." She shook her head, looking up at Jack. "Only some."

More black, drippy streaks from Stephen. "Mostly, it was a mess."

Guilt twisted up Emily's trembling lip. Her jet-black eyebrows arched up in sorrow. "And then they all started throwing up."

"Horror from both ends!" Micha sobbed.

Emily shook her head and cried out. "I never almost felt so bad in my whole life!"

At last, their confession ended, and it wasn't followed by dark lamentations on how the weight of guilt pressed upon their mortal souls, but rather, for a moment, they were simply children. Guilt-ridden children, sobbing their apologies to nobody in particular. These truly repentant kids didn't know what to make of it when Jack chuckled and then laughed, and finally snorted, and then grew hysterical…crossing his legs, pounding on his thigh. "I'm gonna pee my pants!" he laughed to tears. The Goth kids looked to one another. They sniffled. Their sobs subsided. Stephen and Emily forced a chuckle or two, and all were bewildered. "That's pretty naughty," Jack said, catching his breath. He thought a moment. "But I don't know if that deserves the wrath of Krampus." He stared at Kevin, still asleep and still believing their secret was a secret that mattered little. "Maybe Naughty means something different to Santa and Krampus?"

"It really wasn't all that funny," Ash grumbled at Jack before snapping at the Goth-kids. "And for the record! Everyone! Everyone knows it was you. So you can tell Kevin nobody *squealed*." She mocked Kevin by shaking her head with wide eyes.

Jack stepped up to her. "You weren't part of this?"

"No," Stephen explained it simply. "She's lame." Ash threw him a look that quickly fixed his tone. "Kevin says she's lame. A poseur."

Jack got so wrapped up in figuring out what it meant that she wasn't part of their summer fun and yet was still on the list, that he didn't pay any attention to the banter.

"You even know what a poseur is?" Ash asked. "It's when you're pretending to be something you're not. I've never considered myself Goth, but we still used to be friends." Emily's sad eyes grew more sad, as if to say for her part she was sorry they were no longer friends. "And just because Kevin's being a jerk, doesn't mean you all have to be jerks."

"But, then…" Jack thought. "Why are you on Krampus' Naughty list?"

And with a sharp look, Ash retorted, "That's what I aim to find out."

# 8 - ELF ON THE FRIGGING SHELF!

Jack, of course, wasn't the only elf delivering that night. Unlike Jack, and because of Jack, Feliz wasn't delivering coal to any house Christmas Eve…just presents for the Nice kids. But something odd struck Feliz at Amy Doohan's house. After spriting about the room and piling presents under the tree, he bounded for the fireplace to find not one, but two stockings—one for Amy, and the other for Sally.

"Amy?" Feliz scratched his head and pulled out his taped-up scroll of Nice kids. "I don't have an Amy," he said. "Just Sally."

"What's that?" Mickie asked through the headset.

"I only brought presents for Sally. We don't have an Amy on the list."

At North Pole Headquarters, Mickie frowned at Candi. "Maybe Amy is on our Naughty List?" Candi caught his frown from a side glance, and guilt tugged her attention to the opposite direction. She clacked at the keyboard, feigning cluelessness while pretending to be busy. She ran her fingers through her hair to pull a drape of blond and green between herself and his gaze. Her stack of crumpled-up snack wrappers and empty drink cans had grown, spilling over the edge of her desk and onto the floor.

"We don't have any Naughty kids," Feliz shot back.

"I know we don't have any Naughty kids," Mickie snapped. Candi winced, clacking faster. Still, despite all the weirdness of this Christmas Eve, and despite the rightful suspicion being thrown at her, she found this a more entertaining way to spend the holiday than her usual fare of trying to drag Jack out to Thimble's for drinks.

Feliz tossed a gift under the tree. "I'll just leave her a present anyway. Gotta keep moving."

"Don't forget the milk and cookies," Mickie reminded him, for that was one of the jobs of the Helpers.

But Feliz hit a wall…a wall of sugar cookie nausea. "Ay-yi-yi. I just can't do another cookie. No wonder Santa's so fat! I'll just take them with me."

"Be sure to leave some crumbs so they know Santa ate the cookies."

"How do crumbs help anything?"

"Look," Mickie said, glancing through a homemade booklet of sorts. "Mrs. Claus put it in her notes. It's protocol. Make it look like Santa drank some milk, too."

"Dude," Feliz grumbled. "You know warm milk is the worst? Not taking another sip."

"Just pretend."

"Fine! Could really go for a peppermint ale about now."

"And leave crumbs in the glass."

"Sheesh!" Feliz hopped onto the couch towards the cookies and milk that had been left on the end table. But, much to his dismay, there on the end table, Feliz was greeted by a note for Santa, held up by Elf On The Shelf. Feliz gasped. "Elf on the frigging shelf!" Feliz snatched the doll. "That is an offensive stereotype!" He throttled the doll, and upon catching his own reflection, gave pause. Taking in his own ridiculous outfit—the elf-sized Santa hat, the elf-sized Santa uniform, the elf-sized Santa boots. A whispered "freak" escaped his lips as he dropped the doll. And then a curious anger welled up inside. "I'm an elf on a shelf! I'm a frigging stereotype!"

Jack was right about all of them being freaks. And this gave Feliz a bit of a meltdown. The kind of meltdown that required more than a peppermint ale or two at the Nutcracker Tavern. Upset that he was a frigging stereotype along the likes of Elf On The Shelf, Feliz raided the bathroom drawers for make-up to give Shelfie a make-over. The rosiness of Shelfie's cheeks was paled-over; eyeliner made his eyes angrier, and a thin hoop earring now hung from his ear. He etched "Krampus" in black marker across Shelfie's back, and attempted to tear some of his clothes, but when cutting through the pants with toenail scissors, he was met with stuffing that poofed from Shelfie's leg. "Oh, that ain't good," Feliz said, thinking. "But not that you don't deserve it!" He quickly rummaged the drawers of the bathroom sink and found a sewing kit and then patched him up with a few stitches, but then had the thought that if Jack were to do this he would have cut a proper gash. A few shades of eyeshadow painted into the wound fixed that as he blended purples and greens with a tiny bit of red lipstick until it looked properly gangrenous. And when Feliz was done, he looked at Shelfie and thought the only thing that looked out of place was that stereotypical elf smile.

His reflection in the bathroom mirror didn't smile, for it was Shelfie who got the makeover. Feliz still looked like a stereotype. The very thing, he now understood, that Jack had railed against for so long. So he took the white powder puff and slowly dragged it across his cheek, smudging away the natural rosiness into an empty canvas. And the dark eyeliner made his eyes as angry as Jack's. And a peculiarly purplish shade of lipstick made his mouth seem like the night; dark, hollow, yet full of endless possibility. He tore a few rips in his red pant legs and cut a few angry holes in his Santa coat, but he smartly avoided giving himself gashes as he had done to Shelfie. Now he perhaps looked like he was ready to pledge the Jolly Dead Brigade. But, of course, the Jolly Dead Brigade had no makeup and dress requirements…membership was about carrying a certain angstiness inside one's heart. And, most times, it wasn't even about that.

But as Feliz returned Shelfie to the plate of cookies, and Feliz replaced the note for Santa with a new one that read "Greetings from the Krumpus!" a popcorn spark flashed in the fireplace. Feliz turned to the fireplace, curious. He jumped back into the branches of the Christmas tree as more popcorn flashes bounced here and there until a fire roared to life. And from the flames emerged a dark, shadowy figure. Feliz quietly stepped back further into the branches, peering out from behind a bauble.

Krampus!

Jack's idol paused, stretching out a long and crooked finger to move the bauble, exposing Feliz. Feliz gulped, taking in the twisted horns and hairy body. Krampus' face was slightly flat so that his nose was a bulldog snout. One hairy leg was human with a clawed foot; the other was goat-like with a cloven hoof. His long tongue slithered out and flicked the air. "Krampus?!" Feliz gasped, as his right eye twitched and then…he wet himself.

Krampus chuckled, snatching Shelfie in his clawed hand. He turned it over, appreciating Feliz's handiwork. "Jackie Rumpus," he growled, dropping the "Krumpus" doll back onto the table and disappearing into the dark of the hall. Feliz stood petrified, breathing shallow with his heart racing in his ears.

At North Pole Headquarters, Mickie repeated the word he couldn't believe he had just heard. "Krampus? What do you mean he's real?" And this yanked Candi's attention…*what?* Mickie shrugged at her, wide-eyed. She slid over to him and yanked his headset aside so that both their heads were painfully wedged in. Feliz uttered a frightened whisper, "He knows Jackie."

Candi bolted upright. The headset snapped against Mickie's temple. He cowered and rubbed the side of his head. "What do you mean he knows Jackie?" she shouted, and all the Helpers on duty turned to her. "This isn't funny, Rooney!"

Feliz hid behind the tree, recoiling from Candi's shouting. "Ay, yi, yi," he whispered. "He's coming!" He drew in a deep breath and held it there, as if doing so would make him invisible, safe.

Krampus strode through the living room, chuckling, as Amy screamed from his handbasket. From the fireplace, a reingoyle poked out from the flames—with its twisted devil horns for antlers and thin bat-like wings. Krampus paused before it and scolded it like a bad dog. It whimpered from its master's glare and retreated into the fire. Krampus followed after, disappearing into the fireplace before the flames extinguished, along with Amy's screams for Mommy and Daddy.

Feliz waited until he could hold his breath no more and then stepped out. His whole body trembled. "I'm done," he said, wheezing a few deep breaths. "I'm done! I'm done! I'm done! I wanna come home!"

"You can't come home," Mickie reminded him. "Kids are counting on you. Santa's counting-"

"I'm coming home." Just then, the white wisps swirled in from the fireplace. "What the-" Ephemeral fog swirled about him. His eyes grew wide. His arms went up. The wind enveloped him, freezing him in a crystalline cocoon before rushing back up into the fireplace. Feliz teetered, slammed forward against the floor and then got sucked up into the chimney along with the Krumpus doll.

# 9 - SECRET SANTA

Santa, of course, was not about to let the Flyers out into the world without some sort of aid…aid beyond what the Helpers could offer. Normally, the job of minding the giant snow globe in Santa's office went to Crusty. And, normally, Crusty had only one Flyer to mind…and that was Santa Claus himself. This year, with all the Flyers and Helpers out helping, and Santa having nothing to do, he decided to mind the globe himself, and he watched over his Flyers with a fierce gaze.

Presently, Feliz's scene in Amy Doohan's living room played out among the misty swirls inside the globe. Santa's index finger, pressed against the glass, commanded the ephemeral fog. And, just then, the white wisps that unfell and unbroke and froze things inside cocoons, they retreated up towards Santa's finger and left Amy's living room pristine, with no sign of Feliz or the Krumpus doll. Santa paused and sighed in disappointment.

"Snowballs," he grumbled. He absently knocked a knuckle against the glass, causing the fog to flash and turn into the proper snow of a snow globe. It swirled about and finally settled on the bottom before a gentle fog started to rise and again fill the space. Santa turned to the list of Flyers on his desk and crossed off Feliz's name. Only Jack, at the top of the list, remained. Now, mind you, none of the other Flyers had the experience of wetting themselves hysterical after meeting Krampus; nor did they make the unfortunate mistakes that caused Christmas to destroy living rooms, but as Santa had watched throughout the night, he found subtle reasons to worry that something was missing in all his Flyers.

Buddy, for example, completely ignored a drunkard who had passed out in an alley, and who groggily assumed he was hallucinating as he caught glimpses of the elf darting from one apartment window to the next. While delivering coal to a particularly naughty Elise Strombaur, Tinsel didn't consider that perhaps her family could have used additional coal on account of the frigid weather and lack of firewood. And when Noel didn't find anyone at the house of Pierre Laurent—on the Nice list—he simply left the gift in the empty living room. None of these elves had done anything wrong, mind you. They actually did exactly what they were supposed to do, but nothing more. And most elves lacked something that might incite them to do anything more than they had been instructed. They lacked something that might see them caring for a man sleeping in an alley, or to be generous with the coal, or perhaps try to find a child and his family at a shelter a few blocks away. They lacked something. Something special. And, despite all his flaws, Santa was realizing that this special quality—whatever it was—was not lacking in Jack, who had taken the briefest of detours to spread Christmas cheer to a frazzled and harried Patricia James, a single mom to whom Christmas often overwhelmed. He rapped his fingers against the list and then got up, bumping into The Missus as he exited his office. "Can you alert the team in the barn?" he asked her. "Feliz's team should be arriving shortly."

Mrs. Claus nodded. "An accident?" Santa merely groaned at her as he walked away. "Where are you headed?"

"Infirmary. This was a bad idea."

"Is Feliz okay?" she called.

"Aye," he nodded, never looking back. "He will be."

At his workstation, Mickie panicked. "Feliz?" he called. His Flyer had stopped responding, and according to the protocols set forth by Mrs. Claus, the appropriate response was to not panic. "Feliz!" He and Candi turned to one another, frightened.

Candi checked the radar app on her workstation. Jack hadn't moved any. "Jackie?" She waited for as long as she could stand, which wasn't very long at all. "JACK!"

Jack winced and recoiled. "Would you please stop shouting?"

"I need you to come home," she said.

"What? Why?"

"Krampus is real!"

"Duh," Jack smiled, adding a little sing-song jab himself.

Candi slapped her palm against the top of her workstation as if doing so could slap some sense into Jack's head. "No, I mean he's really real!"

Jack just could not understand the urgency in her voice. "I know! Been telling you that for years."

"Rumplemints, Jackie! He knows who you are!" Her fists now balled up in front of her chest, shaking.

The thought of Krampus, his idol, knowing who he was, made Jack feel all sorts of proud. "Krampus knows me?!"

"That doesn't sound like a good thing, Rumpus!"

Jack winced again. "Shouting…"

Candi paced, tensing up—frustrated. She finally threw down her headset, clenching her fists even tighter. "Crumpets!"

To which, the unfortunately-named Crumpet turned from her workstation. "Yep?"

"No, crumpets! Not Crumpet. Crumpets!"

As she stormed away, Mickie called, "Where are you going?"

"Uh…" she paused, "biobreak. Be right back." But Candi knew she wasn't going to be right back. She had to keep Jack from meeting Krampus.


Santa chatted with the Elf Nurse in the bright-white clinic. "Feliz Navidad," he nodded. "Should be arriving shortly." And with that, a red and green light poofed in the fireplace. Still encased in ice, Feliz shot out and slid across the room, spinning until stopped by Santa's boot. The ice quickly melted as Feliz started screaming, hysterical. "Feliz!" Santa called. "Feliz, Fel-" Frustrated, Santa hit him with a sleep-ball, and sighed, thinking while tapping the end of his nose. "Keep him out 'til morning." He left, but turned back in the doorway, crinching up his nose as if smelling something disgusting. "Oh, and you might want to get him out of those clothes."

Santa thumped through the halls of Headquarters, hobbling with his cane clicking against the floor, mumbling to himself some curse about being too old. The clicking cane stopped at Candi's unmanned workstation. Santa blinked as if half-expecting that the blinks would magically make her appear. He turned to Mickie, who sat, staring off into the windows to the cold snowy night. Twiddling his thumbs as he mumbled to himself, "We're not panicking. We're not panicking."

"Where's Candi?" Santa asked, giving Mickie a start.

"I'm not panicking!" He twisted so fast and hard he might have given himself whiplash.

"Feliz is fine," Santa assured. "I brought him home."

"Oh." Mickie's shoulders relaxed. "That's good."

"Candi?"

"Bathroom. I think." And he thought. "Been a while."

"Any updates on Jackie?" Mickie shrugged. "And what are you doing?"

Mickie looked about as if he were being accused of doing *some*thing. "Nothing," he insisted. "I didn't know what to do."

Santa put his hands to his hips. "But sitting there…doing nothing. That seems like the right thing?"

"I don't. Um…" Mickie's eyes darted left and right. "What should I do?"

An annoyed sigh followed The Santa Look, which was missed on Mickie. "Nothing, Mickie," Santa grumbled as he clicked away. "Just keep doing what you're doing." Mickie watched him huff away, then dutifully returned to doing nothing. The snowflakes tumbled down outside, and Mickie's mind wandered out the windows and up, and up, and up, to where snow became snow and perhaps had not even begun to fall just yet. To where flakes had just formed and maybe just delicately held onto the sky before finally letting go.

Candi, on the other hand, had no time for a wandering mind. She speed-walked through the hallway, startled upon hearing Feliz shrieking in the distance, which propelled her outside and into the cold nighttime wind. She rushed past the Kettlekarts that zipped along, hiding from the crowd outside Thimble's, past the edge of town and out to the reindeer barn. Once there, she grabbed a familiar brown saddle and rushed straight to Rudolph's pen.

"Okay, Rudy…just like always, but fast-" She dropped the saddle and looked about. To her surprise, her favorite reindeer had gone missing. "-er." She stepped into the middle of the pen and turned about, half-expecting a red glow to materialize. "Rudolph?" A sigh slipped from her as her shoulders drooped and she pondered her next move…Noxen. Candi peered around Rudolph's gate and way down towards the dark end of the barn, to where a lone reindeer had been kept apart from the others, from where a silvery light might spark  and shimmer before fizzling. "Noxen," she repeated to herself, this time out loud with a determined nod.

Snatching the saddle and sneaking towards that light, Candi barely wondered if taking Noxen was a wise move. It felt too necessary. She had flown with him a couple times, and as far as one could be friends with a reindeer, she considered him as such. It would all depend on his mood, which she carefully assessed as she stepped into his pen. Noxen had been known for his brand of foul mood, and more specifically how dismal he made others feel in his presence. He looked like a menace, standing taller than the other reindeer, thick with muscle, sporting a black hide and even blacker mane that seemed to suck the very happiness from one's soul. His antlers twisted about, looking like the gnarled branches of some ancient tree. And his eyes, they shimmered with a silver light that often mirrored his fleeting moods. Despair often overcame those who first met him, driving affected elves to their knees, sobbing and gasping as they struggled to understand the onslaught of sadness. But for those who could see past the darkness that enshrouded Noxen, the despair was just as fleeting as the reindeer's moods. A few, such as Candi and Jack, had never even experienced the effect.

Santa wasn't so lucky, and the first time he met the beast, he collapsed to tears, wailing like some child who had discovered he was on the Naughty List for the tenth straight year. Santa resigned Noxen to the dark corner, away from the elves who worked the barn, away from the other reindeer, and he told himself he would figure out just what to do with Noxen…but he never did. Jack and Candi would often sneak Noxen out to give him a bit of exercise and keep him company, and they even managed to help him make a few reluctant friends with the other reindeer. But Santa? He never got over his first encounter.

"Noxen?" Candi began, welcomed with a silvery glint in his eyes. "I know we've never flown outside The Pole, but can you help me? There's no one faster than you, and Jackie's gonna meet Krampus."

She patted him on his side as he grunted and stomped his foot, eyes shimmering as he pushed her with his snout, right to the floor.

"Gentle!" she admonished him, climbing to her feet and brushing off the hay. More grunts. Another stomp. "What do you mean, so? If they meet, then the perma-swear means nothing." She shook her head. "He won't come home."

He nudged her again, this time more gently, as the barn doors threw open and a cold gust of wind swirled up dust and straw. Candi peeked from the pen at the elves leading Feliz's reindeer team inside from the night, before she turned back with a whisper. "You knew Krampus is real?"

"Any idea what happened to Feliz?" one of the elves asked.

Noxen brayed, moving uneasily. "Shh…" Candi whispered, calming him.

"Not a clue," said the other elf. "I heard something about Krumpus, but-"

"Can't imagine him and Jackie going at it again on Christmas Eve!"

"Exactly!"

Silence overtook the elves as they worked to remove the reindeer team's harnesses until one of the elves shared a thought. "You don't…think…maybe," he trailed off at the absurdity he was considering. "Maybe it was…*Krampus*?"

Suddenly, all the inside of the barn momentarily went dark as it seemed all light had been sucked away, and in the darkness that followed, two bolts of silvery-blue lightning spidered-out in either direction as the barn doors threw open again, the wind rushed in, and the lights all felt like they had whipped back into place. A silver streak shot high into the night as the elves turned back to the doors and Feliz's reindeer grew uneasy.

"What was that?"

The second elf went to the doors and looked out into the cold with a shrug. "Probably just the wind."

"Did you not see the lighting?" the first elf asked, incredulous that the second had missed such a detail.

That silver streak, of course, was Noxen and Candi, shooting higher and higher into the night, to where snow became snow, and hovered so delicately before letting its grip slip. "I didn't know you could do that!" Candi laughed, patting the side of his mane. "I thought your magic was just bad moods!" They dashed over land. And dashed over ocean. Over cities and lakes, cars, and the suburban tackiness that was Christmas. Candi leaned in to urge Noxen on faster. "Homestretch, Noxen!" she shouted. "Everything you got!" And the silver streak brayed and shot faster over the Midwestern skies.

# 10 – CAREFUL WHAT YOU WISH FOR

It didn't take long for Jack to realize the flaw in his new plan of sitting around and waiting for Krampus to find him…it was all the sitting around and all the waiting. He fought off boredom by building a model of the reindeer barn on the bar top. The kids all watched in awe as his hands moved, rapid-fire, twisting cocktail napkins, straws, toothpicks and other random items into something amazing. Nobody was more impressed than Ash, who imagined all the incredible things she might build if she could move like that. The finished model wasn't red but was otherwise a pretty accurate representation of an old and weathered barn that couldn't possibly house hordes of reindeer. "That spider thingy," Jack said, stepping back from his creation, but still looking into it as if he might actually see a reindeer move about. "You make that?" He turned to Ash, whose gaze moved between him and the barn and back again as she nodded. "I bet you'd make a great elf." Stephen arched his eyes, wondering if that was a compliment or not, but Ash didn't question his words.

Her appreciative smile appeared and then quickly faded, much like the brief, brilliant glow of a heavenly meteor.

Kevin groaned back to life.

"Hey!" Micha looked down at Kevin, speaking to Jack. "Mister."

"Jack," he nodded back, turning his model about the bar top to check if the detail on the north side of the barn was right. One hand scratched at his head while the other absently reached for a stack of cardboard coasters. Ash watched, fascinated, as Jack bent and folded the squares into a vehicle of sorts, imagining what the real thing must look like, sound like, how it moved, and never guessing it was Jack's version of the modified Kettlekart that hauls manure to Hollyberry Farms.

"Mister Jack," Micha began again. "Kevin isn't dead."

"Undead bliss," Emily considered. "A vampire?"

The thought of any one of them, especially Kevin, being a vampire should have been ridiculous, let alone a bit terrifying, but Stephen couldn't contain his excitement at the thought. "A vampire?! Cool!" And then he remembered how uncool it was to find something so cool. "I mean," he shrugged. "Whatever."

Jack sighed, turning the kind of look to the Goth kids that Santa usually held for Jack...The Santa Look. Sometimes The Santa Look was a warning, at other times it was just an expression of frustration. The version Jack conjured was an observation and a question just the same...*are you possibly that stupid?* "I just put him to sleep is all," he shrugged.

Micha's eyes reddened raw from sobbing—not the kind of shrill cry that elvish ears can't tolerate, but more of a slow, whimpering sob. "I want to go home."

"Sorry," Jack said, and he truly was sorry. "We just have to wait."

"For what?" Ash asked. She already knew for what, but had hoped Jack would let a few more details slip.

Kevin jerked awake. "Get me off my back, you hobbit!" Jack hopped off the bar stool, and in a sing-song tone suggested the Goth leader say please. "I'll please kick your-" But before Kevin finished his threat, Jack rocked him upright and stood upon Kevin's knees.

"You're not very nice," Jack observed.

Ash sniggered, "Ya think?"

Kevin turned his anger on her. "Who asked you?"

"Emily Dickinson!" Jack snapped. Popcorn sparks yanked his attention upstairs, followed by a hot flash of fire, and then…a shadow! As if Jack's beaming smile had taken hold of his whole self, and its happiness overwhelmed his body, Jack trembled with the force of a thousand grins sparked from the purest joy. He hopped up and down on Kevin's knees. "He's here! He's here!" he exclaimed, his voice shaking.

Kevin looked up. "Who's here?"

Ash's eyes grew wide and darted up to the top of the stairs. She craned her neck down, foolishly trying to peek around the corner of the stairwell, as if light could bend to her will.

"Krampus!" Jack giggled. His idol was mere feet from him! His Christmas wish of many years, finally coming true! He trembled. His throat fought off an excited scream so that merely a squeak had escaped and Jack had nearly passed out from the pressure in his neck. And then…he all-out fangirled. A shriek that surprised even him sprang from the center of his chest and radiated out to his shoulders, shooting down his extended arms, and seemingly escaping him through his quivering fingertips.

And, of course, finding anything so cool, was just so very uncool for Stephen. "Get a grip, man."

Ash continued to crane her neck, trying to grab a look upstairs.

In her monotone drab, Emily confessed how she fangirled once. "When I met Andy from Black Veiled Brides. I got all tangled up in my cloak. Knocked over both of us."

"I'm embarrassed for you," Stephen said to both Jack and Emily.

"Then security tackled us. Broke my nose." And then, as if it were a crowning achievement, she added, "My nose bled all over Andy from Black Veiled Brides! Ruined my cloak, though."

Krampus' legs stepped down onto the stairway, and Jack paused. He was about to meet his idol. And he didn't want his idol to see him fangirling. Why…everyone probably fan-girls when they meet Krampus, he thought. He had to calm down, get it together, be cool. "Be cool," he said to himself, and then—poof!—he disappeared behind the bar to compose himself.

The kids watched Krampus descend, and when they got a load of his full form, a towering dark creature in the basement, they got their freak on. At first, Jack thought they, too, were fangirling, but it wasn't an excited scream. Jack's excitement blinded him to their terror. All but Kevin tried to scoot away, stuck in their seats so that Kevin sat silent and alone.

Krampus rounded the bottom of the stairs, crouched over on account of a low ceiling and his long legs. He first caught sight of Ash scooting her chair backward, trembling, eyes fixed on his. "Ashanti Omondi," he growled, slow and deep, and as if him saying her name was a command, she suddenly stilled. "You've been naughty." He swooped her up, chair and all, and stuffed her into his crowded basket. She was barely able to gasp as he did so.

"Kevin Mahoney." Krampus twisted his neck as he slowly turned his eyes toward his new prey. "You've been naughty." The Goth kids screamed as Krampus swooped up Kevin—also chair and all—and stuffed him into his basket. And to Krampus' surprise, standing in Kevin's space, was Jack, smiling brightly. "Jackie Rumpus?" Krampus crooked his neck. "You've been naughty."

And Krampus surprised Jack with a chuckle, swiping for him. "What?!" Jack shouted, hopping away in time. Krampus' empty fist knocked over Emily and Stephen, who were KO'ed, down for the count, out like lights— and not at all in the sleep-ball sense. Krampus had hit them hard. "No!" Jack shouted, waving his pleading hands. "Don't hurt them!"

"You're coming with me!" Another swipe and a miss. Micha's sobs quieted as he got knocked out against the other wall. Jack paused on their limp forms, heartbroken.

"No!" he shouted at his idol. "Not like this!"

"Oh? You say."

"I want to help you!"

"Krampus doesn't need help." He frowned at the absurdity of anyone suggesting otherwise.

"But I can get the Naughty kids for you." Jack surveyed the bodies, keeping one eye on Krampus. "Like these. And you don't have to hurt them."

Krampus stepped forward, causing Jack to take a few steps back. "I didn't need you to get them." Krampus swiped for him, missed, and smashed the reindeer barn.

Jack looked at its ruins, pained and realizing, "I really am on your Naughty List." How all of his schemes and plans suddenly felt so very selfish—a betrayal to all that was Christmas. To these Goth kids. To all the other Helpers and Flyers. To Santa himself.

Jack's flying Helper circled high above the cul-de-sac, zeroing in on her target. She pointed to where Jack's team perched upon the rooftop of Kevin's house. "Over there!" Candi shouted. Noxen dove, and as they neared the house, Candi added "We're going in!" But in all the Christmas Eve stories Noxen had heard about Santa over the years, "going in" to the chimney was never a thing…the reindeer always landed on top of the house…why would they ever go inside with Santa? The reindeer objected, locked his legs and tried to put all the stops on. "Relax," Candi said, rubbing his neck. "Jackie says it can be done." And as Noxen skidded through the air, he swirled into the chimney sideways.

They suddenly found themselves spinning through Hell—Krampus' domain. Fire, flying reingoyles, trolls way down below on the rocky cliffs. Candi gripped at his mane in fear, and on one of their spins about, she managed to catch a glimpse of a fireplace burning up above. "Up, Noxen!" she shouted. The dark beast managed to still the spinning, shook off the dizzy, and shot up to the fireplace.

Poof! Candi and Noxen tumbled out of the fireplace, still burning with Krampus' open portal. Candi flew off the reindeer and knocked over the flat screen tv. Noxen, meanwhile, rolled into a sofa table and shattered family photos and knickknacks, landing face-to-face with a stuffed animal representation of Rudolph, wearing a green football jersey with a large *01* across its chest, playing for the *Reindeer Games*. The reindeer blinked his confusion at the stuffed avatar. Candi rubbed her head, nauseous. "Oh, that did not feel good." She helped Noxen to his feet, rubbing his sides. "Are you okay, Noxen?" A loud crash from the basement startled her.

And that crash was actually a smash, as Krampus kept swinging for Jack and missing. Jack hopped from the bar top. Smash! He hopped onto the sofa. Smash! "But I wanted to run away with you!" Jack shouted, hopping onto the end table. "Be your helper." Smash! He realized why Santa never delivered on his wish. And he realized he misplaced his idolization. And he felt angry and hurt, and betrayed by his own heavy heart. "You were my hero!" he sniffled.

And this caught Krampus' attention. He stopped. Dropped the basket. "Hero?"

Jack caught his breath, with angry sad tears of disappointment welling up, realizing the absurdity of his wish. "I wanted to come live with you." Krampus cocked his head askew and thought. His long tongue flickered out, went up his nose and cleaned out snot, thoroughly grossing out Jack. "That's just," Jack swallowed. "Oh, nasty."

"You can show me where the North Pole is."

"The Pole?" Jack wiped away a tear. "You don't know where it is?"

"Polar Magic," Krampus thought. "Confounds it." And it almost looked as though Krampus had calmed into someone Jack could like. The Christmas demon's shoulders slackened. The furious tension in his face melted away. The fierceness of his eyes mellowed, exposing someone thoughtful. With purpose. A mission and a reason. But it was a fleeting glimpse of someone Krampus might have once been.

When Kevin struggled inside the basket, all of Krampus' rage returned and he kicked the basket across the room. "Quiet!" he shouted, and the viciousness of the action weighed on Jack. He lamented on the other kids, passed out from their blows. He needed to find a way to keep them safe. Jack kept eying the basket, trying to find a way to snatch it from Krampus.

"W-why do you want to find The Pole?"

Krampus spat. "Because Christmas should be mine!" He jutted his face into Jack's so that Jack tumbled backward. And then, Krampus smiled, seeing Candi running down the stairs. He rushed to retrieve his basket.

"Jackie!" she called.

"Candi Kane!" Krampus growled, hurrying up the stairs and stuffing her into his basket before she could realize what was happening. She shrieked as he added, "You've been naughty!"

"Jackie!" she cried.

And Jack bounded to his feet and up the stairs. "Candi!"

Candi tumbled out of the basket, scurrying away across the living room floor. Krampus chased after, pausing in fascination upon seeing Noxen standing in the middle of the room. The black coat, dark mane, twisted antlers that looked like ancient and twisted tree branches, the silver shimmer of his eyes… Krampus gasped, "What is this magnificent beast?!" Noxen looked like he belonged with him in Hell.

Jack lobbed a sleep-ball at Krampus, jarring him from his gaping stare, but aside from that, the sleep-ball had no effect. Jack then lobbed a barrage of sleep-balls—all of which had a similar no-effect except to annoy Krampus as a glowing-sparkly-wet mess bounced off him and piled about his feet.

"Weak Polar Magic," Krampus chuckled.

"Do something else," Candi suggested, climbing onto Noxen's back, to which Jack shouted that he didn't know what else to do. And then, just as they did in the reindeer barn, all the lights of the room got sucked into Noxen's black mane, casting the room in momentary darkness, and then snapping into place as two silvery-blue bolts shot from Noxen's eyes and blinding Krampus. He charged, head-butting Krampus to the gut. Krampus threw back, smashing into the fireplace and destroying the mantle—pictures, stockings, and knickknacks all scattered. Candi's grip gave, and she tumbled up and over Noxen's head, bouncing off Krampus and onto the floor.

Krampus shook off the blow, snarled, and retreated into the fireplace.

Jack and Candi breathed a moment of rest, and just as they thought they had won, Krampus reached through the flames and grabbed Candi by the ankle.

"Jackie!" she shouted. And she scrawled and kicked, but was yanked and dragged backward into the flames. Jack dove to her and just missed. They scrambled to lock hands. "Jackie!" she shouted again.

Her screams faded into the flames.

The flames faded into dark.

"Candi!" he called, aghast, taking in a few bated breaths. He looked about. A few more breaths. What to do, what to do?! He climbed to his feet and surveyed the fireplace. "Open sesame?" Nothing. "Grus vom Krampus?!" More nothing only agitated him. "Krampusnacht! Krampuskarten! Krampus schnapps!" He stomped, kicked, punched and finally screamed a blood-curdling yell, collapsing onto the floor in tears. His Christmas wish, his only Christmas wish, the one

Christmas wish for this year and many years before…took away his Candi. It was his fault, he sobbed, too overwhelmed to hear Noxen scratching his hoof on the floor and sniffling for attention.

When scratching and sniffling failed to snap Jack from his misery, the reindeer pushed his cold nose into Jack's neck, shoving him sideways to the floor. Jack coughed to stifle his cries, took in the beast, and appreciated the comfort, such as it was. He scratched Noxen's muzzle, and freak-to-freak, he sniffled, "Hey, freak." And the freak's eyes shimmered soft and dim, giving Jack an idea.

Santa!

Jack rushed into the kitchen, frantically rummaging through drawers until he finally found what was needed—a pen, a pad of paper, and an envelope. The chair legs at the table squealed, and he hopped up, standing on the chair and speaking as he wrote:

*Dear Santa,*

*Every year, we get one Christmas wish. Just one. And every year you never come through. It's your fault that I-*

"Gah!" he grimaced at his own words, tearing off the sheet from the pad, crumpling it and tossing it away. Gotta be good, he thought. Gotta be good. He tugged at his hair and thought.

*Dear Santa,*

*I know that every year I wish for the same thing, and you never give me what I ask for. And I know that this must sound like I am asking you for the same thing again. But it's different. I need your help. Krampus took Candi! Please open the door to Krampus so I can get her back. I've been a good elf this year.*

He thought, swallowed, and finally scratched out his last sentence. Santa would know the truth.

*I've been mostly a good elf.*

And again, he thought and scratched away his words. And sorrowful tears welled up and trickled down. Why was it so hard for him to be just a regular, jolly elf? Why did he hate The Pole so much? Did he really hate The Pole? Or, did The Pole hate him? The cold, he hated. Making toys, red and green, his stupid elf name, Feliz Navidad and Mickie Rooney. All these thoughts he pondered as he wrote what finally felt honest.

*I'm sorry I'm such a bad elf. Please help me anyway.*

Tearful, he stuffed the letter into the envelope and scribbled: Santa Claus, North Pole, URGENT! Into the cold outside, he trekked, leaving tiny footprints on top of the new snow, to the mailbox at the end of the driveway. As soon as he shut the door on his letter, a brilliant puff of pastel-colored light knocked him onto his back and shot the letter high and fast, like a comet, into the glistening dark sky with a long sparkly trail.

# 11 - DUNKELSTIMMA

A gleeful Krampus bounded down a twisting, rocky path that had sprung from the other side of Kevin's fireplace. To one side was a cliff wall, and to the other a sheer drop. Horrid creatures screeched and howled in the vast, fire-filled, space. Here and there, eerie wisps of steam rose from the mostly barren ground and drifted through the branches of the few dead or slowly dying trees that dotted the landscape, stretching and pulling into long, bony ghostly hands that looked as if searching for a lost soul to snatch further into the abysmal depths.

The inside of Krampus' basket was cramped and dark, not quite of the same sort of magic as Santa's sack, though it still held more space inside than it appeared to on the outside. Hands and feet squirmed and pushed and kicked, and children cried out for their moms and dads. An occasional hand or leg poked outside of the basket, only to get slammed shut upon.

Ash, pressed against the inside of the basket, could feel the leg of Kevin's chair jabbing into her side. She called out for Mhambi, who struggled to push its forward legs together to a point and used that to wedge through the cramped space while pushing with the back legs. "Cut me out."

"You think you could cut me out, too?" Kevin snapped, accidentally causing the chair leg to jab deeper into her leg.

"Why would I help you?" she winced. "You can't even ask nice."

"That was nice!"

As soon as Mhambi had freed her hands, Ash wriggled about and got the chair leg away from her and grabbed a corner of a cloth Mhambi had pried from the backpack. "You ready?" The spider chirped affirmative and then cut a horizontal slit in the side of the basket. But before slipping out, Ash pushed her face under some kid's arms and looked Kevin in the eyes. "Maybe Hell will do you some good," she said. And for as mean as it sounded, and for as hurtful as Kevin took its meaning, it was actually the kindest gesture she could muster up before slipping out the basket, a way of honoring their old friendship. Once Ash had squeezed out, the contents of the basket groaned and resettled and adjusted so that Candi popped, slightly bent, near Kevin's ear. "What just happened?" she asked to nobody in particular.

"Ash just escaped," Kevin said.

"What ash?" she asked. "Are we on fire?"

Outside the basket, Ash landed with a roll, wrapping herself in a dirty tan blanket as she did so, and unfortunately losing her grip on Mhambi. When Krampus felt an ever so slight shift in the weight and contents of his basket, he stopped and turned to see if any of the Naughty kids had managed to escape. But all he saw were rocks on the dirt path, which is exactly what

Ash wanted him to see. But he also saw a robot spider with a glass-like body…which Ash definitely did not want Krampus to see. He stepped toward the thing, which didn't dare attack or stray too far from Ash. He reached down for it, curious, but it chittered a few steps back, and then a few steps to the left, and then a few steps forward between Krampus' legs so now it was behind him.

Krampus turned about, looking down at the thing before finally dismissing it as just another lost toy. He kicked Mhambi over the cliff and continued on his jaunt down the path. From under the blanket, Ash's eyes grew wide, but she didn't dare yell out for her robot friend, or come out from under the blanket just yet. She waited for Krampus to bound out of sight before coming out of hiding and scrambling to the ledge, to where Mhambi hovered about eight feet below with all arms outstretched in full-on drone mode.

"Oh!" Ash exclaimed. "Thank goodness." Although it looked like Mhambi was merely hiding, the spider was simply trying to not fall and crash onto the rocks way down below. And while hovering and spinning about, it had honed in on the very reason Ash intended to meet Krampus. Mhambi chirped to let Ash know, but Ash was trembling with fearful excitement and how this adventure had turned. "I knew he was real! I just didn't realize he was so…" More chirps and flashes broke her thoughts. "Oh, right!" Ash exclaimed, swiping through the screen on her smartphone wristwatch, to an app she had written that could better translate the chirps and whistles. "You found Maia? Already?!" The screen on her wrist showed a video that spun about as Mhambi moved, zeroing in on the oddest of sights…a German cottage, in the middle of this hellish place, right out of some fairy tale. Its timber frames decorated the exterior in intersecting angles that met at the corners of its windows, which were highlighted with empty flower boxes. Off to its side, amid a garden of sorts that had been squared off with a picket fence, was Maia, perched on a fence post and being used as a decorative gazing ball. She was Mhambi's twin, but without the legs as Ash had added them to Mhambi since Maia's disappearance last Christmas. Yes, Ash's missing friend was another robot, but Ash was an extremely loyal friend…a trait Kevin sorely missed now that they were no longer friends.

Ash had created these sisters of sorts to work together and accomplish tasks, but Maia went missing last Christmas…before Ash had got around to upgrading the spheres, which then simply rolled to get about. She had searched for Maia for days, unable to find her; could not remember where she had seen her last, and just as she was ready to give up the search and just assume that Maia had wandered off somewhere on her own, Ash started to remember things. Vague things of a beast named Krampus. Like a dream of being crammed into a basket and dragged to Hell. A jail maybe. And somewhere along the way, Maia had got lost. She had to come back to rescue Mhambi's sister.

Ash knew—just felt it in her core—that whether she was Naughty or Nice throughout the year was irrelevant. That Krampus would come for her either way. That Krampus likely had come for her year after year. There was something about Ash—something wrong, maybe—certainly something different—just as Jack understood there was something unique about himself that separated him from the other elves. When her former friends all started dressing Goth and listening to their angry music, Ash gave the attitude a try, thinking that perhaps if it felt right, maybe that could explain her angst. But it didn't feel right for her; not for very long, anyway. She let the Goth life mostly slip away as she faded back into her nerdy-tech self. She never considered she'd lose her friends in the process.

Ash looked up from her watch screen and peered toward where Mhambi's camera focused. She could barely make out the house from the distance below. "Do you think you could fly me down? I'm not sure we can make that long walk. Not without getting caught, anyway." Various beasts patrolled the cavernous space. The robot-spider chirped affirmative, but Ash had her doubts. "We never tested how much weight you could carry in drone mode." But Mhambi had little doubt. She bent two legs down so that Ash could hang on her from what looked like the handlebars of a bicycle. Ash stepped to the ledge; looked down and took a deep breath. She wrapped that dirty blanket about her shoulders so as to appear more rock-like, and hopefully more reingoyle-like, before finally reaching up for Mhambi. "Stay close to the cliff wall. I don't want to run into one of those gargoyle things." Mhambi lifted her a couple of feet from the ground and then, as quickly as the ground beneath her feet disappeared, so did Ash's fear. They kept along the cliff wall, taking breaks on tiny precipices whenever Ash's grip grew tired, which became more frequent. On one such break, she started to rummage through her backpack for a patch of rope, thinking she could use it to make a sling, something to sit in or otherwise give her arms a break. But just as she found the rope, the ledge upon which she sat slipped out from under her. She fought every urge to scream as she slid down the cliff wall. Mhambi chased after, but the propellers on two of her arms got tangled up in the blanket, and the two of them tumbled, twisted together. Ash bounced against the rock wall and fell, banged a bit more, couldn't keep her eyes open and coughed from the dust until the blanket had wrapped about the trunk of a long-dead tree that jutted from the side of the cliff. The force of Ash's weight tugged at the roots, to make it seem the trunk would let go of the rock at any moment. "Ugh!" she grunted, the force of the sudden stop pushing the air from her lungs.

Ash swiveled, swinging back and forth from the blanket, watching her backpack continue to tumble and slide down the cliff wall, its contents spilling about. "Don't move," she instructed Mhambi. Two of her legs had gone missing. A third dangled from her body just as precariously as they dangled from the tree. A fourth was trying to cut the other two remaining legs from the blanket. "What to do? What to do?" Ash thought, looking down, around, and up. She wanted to scream for help, but who would help? And the word itself, it just wouldn't come to her.

A long way's up and nearly directly above Ash, Krampus finally arrived to a jail he had carved from a cave in the rock, which was guarded by a troll that had bulldog teeth, thick matted hair, tiny horns, and hairy fawn legs. The child prisoners scattered into the darkness of the cave when Krampus ripped open the barred gate, tossed in a tumbling heap of children and one tiny elf, and slammed shut the door. Even though the children cowered, cried and sobbed, the only sounds that emerged came from the newcomers—who tumbled over one another and struggled to their feet. Candi sprang from the pile and charged the gate…the only one brave enough to do so. When she reached through the bars, sparks shocked her like one of those bug zappers on a summer night. "Son of a…snowballs!" Candi sprang back as the jolt seized every joint in her body.

Krampus chuckled at her pain.

"Where to now, Krampus?!" she spat. "Gonna get your jolly on by kidnapping more kids?" She looked about the dirt and soot-covered rock walls. The children all cowered, except for Kevin. He stood, also looking about, taking in his new surroundings with a mix of fascination and justified concern, absently untangling himself from rope and smashed chair bits from around his limbs. He approached the bars, paying no attention to either Krampus or Candi, feeling the bars and their odd coldness in the heat of the place. "The devils are all really here," he muttered to himself.

Seeing the bars hadn't jolted Kevin, Candi surmised Krampus must have charmed them to keep elves from getting through the spaces between the bars. But why would he do that, she thought, unless Krampus was also taking elves? She quickly glanced about the room…she was the only elf there.

Now that he was back in his space, Krampus felt more relaxed. He moved slowly, jutting and angling as his movements held thought and purpose. "We all have our role in this Christmas pageant, Candi Kane," he said, eerily calm. And he and the elf locked eyes with one another, sizing up the bigness and smallness of one another, before he raised a calm and human hand to the space before him. His eyes rolled up, expectant, and then turned back on Candi. "Dunkelstimma," he whispered.

Candi's eyes went wide. She spun, slapping her hand over Kevin's mouth so that they both tumbled. And a wispy darkness emerged from the newcomers' mouths, smoking and swirling and tumbling into a shadow-ball that rolled through the air to hover at Krampus' palm. Krampus looked at it, fascinated despite it being something he witnessed time and time again, year after year, and he grimaced a gleeful smile as silence gripped all the newcomers. The shadow-ball rose, higher and higher, and merged with a much larger shadow-ball that sounded of nonsense cries and agony. An occasional shape emerged, not unlike a hand, or a face, but only something that was *merely* like a hand or a face—grabbing and shouting.

Krampus' gaze turned from the large shadow-ball back to the cell, and he surveyed the frightened eyes before him. "Terror grips the harshest soul," he said. "Its raging silence takes them home."

Candi charged the bars again, abruptly stopping short of touching them. "Jackie won't leave me here!"

Krampus thrust his face into the bars in a vicious threat. The children all scurried back so that Candi and Kevin, alone, remained. Unmoved. "I'm counting on it!" Krampus shouted, reaching through and yanking her into the bars by the collar. "And you best learn some manners, elf. Pity the spell passes you."

Candi groaned at the pain as sparks shot across her chest, but then she gasped when Kevin did the most unexpected thing. He placed a hand on Krampus' arm.

"Mr. Krampus, sir?" Kevin swallowed, looking about. "I want to go home, please."

Krampus turned to Kevin and chuckled in his surprise. "And you, too? See that, Candi Kane? Kevin wants to go home, *please*." Krampus sighed and released his grip on Candi as if realizing he had let his temper get the best of him. And although Krampus was a demon and not a man, his demeanor changed to that of a gentleman. "You, Kevin, are a quick study. Wants to go home, *please*, at that. You just might go home soon enough." He turned to the troll guarding the jail. "Fetch us a cuppa tea, might you? While we wait for her friends."

The troll scampered as Krampus bounded away.

Candi and Kevin looked to one another, curious. Candi twisted up her face, not believing what she had just heard. "Did he just say fix us a cuppa-"

"Tea," Kevin nodded. "Yes."

# 12 - LETTERS TO SANTA

Santa hobbled through the halls of Headquarters, occasionally rapping his cane against random obstacles in frustration—a garbage can, a copier, a stack of paper reams that some bored elf had stacked into the shape of a Christmas tree. He grumbled the whole while, sometimes stopping to admonish himself for his reckless plan, swiping the cane at another random cubicle wall as if the office had turned into his birthday piñata. Keep in mind, these were elf-sized cubicles; and the walls, they ripped apart like colorful candies. The few elves who hadn't yet left to celebrate jolted upright at their desks, glanced at one another and then to Santa, and quickly scattered as they silently agreed it was time to join the fun at Nutcracker Tavern.

Rushing from the post office, the Postal Elf stepped into Santa's path and nearly got whacked with the cane as he found himself between Santa and a Frosted Moon vending machine. "Ah!" he shouted, cowering from the cane so fast he tripped and fell to the floor.

To which Santa reeled back and gave an "Oh, ho!" Santa caught his bearings and helped his friend to his feet, apologizing all the while and brushing away chocolate remnants of a haphazardly-eaten Polar Bearie that had littered the floor. He looked at the melted chocolate in his palm and wiped it off against his sleeve. And after making sure the Postal Elf was indeed as fine as he insisted, he noticed the letter. "What's this?" he took the envelope and turned it over. "Nobody writes me Christmas Eve."

The Postal Elf wrapped a bony finger around the envelope to point out, "Marked urgent. Most curious."

Santa opened it and read, and with a heavy sigh revealed its author. "Rumpus." He thought a moment, tapping his finger against his nose.

"Do you need my help?" the Postal Elf asked, genuinely concerned, genuinely offering, but secretly hoping that help wasn't needed.

"No, no," Santa said. "You're most overdue for a break." He patted the Postal Elf on the shoulder as he walked on. "Go join the fun over at The Nutcracker." He hobbled along, more thoughtful now, and surprisingly less frustrated. But the problem that had been haunting him for so long had returned. He was tired. But, being Santa, there was no room for being tired. Krampus took Candi? And Jack finally met his idol. He must be scared out of his wits, Santa thought. Jackie meeting Krampus wasn't ever supposed to happen like this.

Santa made his way down a long hallway, dim and empty with row after row of empty cubicles. The elves had all finished their jobs for the year and were off— celebrating at Thimble's, resting at home, or Flying and Helping. At the end of the hallway, he turned to an old and weathered entrance for the old Workshop—back when the Workshop and Headquarters shared the same small space. It was a bit of a museum nowadays. This modern Headquarters facility had been built around it to preserve The Pole's more humble beginnings. Santa stepped through the space, remembering making toys when he was a young elf, the smell of sweat and pine sawdust, how big and magical everything felt, and yet how simple Christmas used to be back in the day. He reached the far end of the Workshop and creaked open an old and heavy wooden door to the outside and stepped into the snow and cold. The wind blew through his clothes as he stepped along a flagstone path to an ancient cottage that didn't look much unlike Krampus' German cottage. Instead of its flowerboxes being filled with soot and ash, however, these flowerboxes overflowed with snow and ice. Some of the older elves congregate here each year on the summer solstice…where about mid-day, arctic poppies magically sprout from the boxes and overflow, forming an icy green, white and yellow carpet about the onlookers' feet. For the older generations, this marks the start of an evening filled with bonfires, dancing, and drinking. Tonight, however, the revelry was elsewhere, in town. Light from the fireplace inside the cottage shimmered in widening swaths onto the snowdrifts below the windows.

Santa stepped up to another large and ancient wooden door and tugged on a rope that jingled a bell inside. And he waited, rubbing his hands on his arms for warmth, wishing he had detoured to get his coat. He jingled the bell again and knocked until the door finally creaked open and Crusty's tired eyes peered outside.

"Santa?" he exclaimed, opening the door wide and ushering him in from the cold.

"Oh, good!" Santa stepped inside, stomping snow off his one shoe into the mat that cheerily welcomed visitors to *Make a Wish*. "You're awake."

"Of course, I'm awake," Crusty said, though he was dressed for bed, wearing his robe and a long striped nightcap. "It's Christmas Eve," he added as if Santa might have forgotten.

"I need you to mind the globe."

"Bring my robe?" Crusty asked as if it were the silliest request, spinning about and looking for it, forgetting that he was already wearing it. "Bring my robe. My robe." He repeated, still circling and searching.

"It's…um…" Santa started to indicate that the robe was about Crusty's shoulders, but instead just corrected the confusion. "No, not your robe. The globe. I need you to mind the globe."

"Oh?!" Crusty wobbled, a bit dizzy from the spinning. "Thought we weren't doing that this year?"

"Change of plans," he said, and the tiredness melted his cold face. Crusty watched him, thoughtful, two pairs of ancient eyes staring into each other.

"Getting to be your time, is it?"

"I reckon so," Santa lamented, swallowing.

"Well," Crusty smiled wide and his eyes brightened, perhaps the only one at The Pole who could understand what had been bothering Santa all this time. "There's no shame in that." He pointed a bony finger to the space between them and then turned to an old and ornate cupboard covered in wood carvings of a forest scene—

an older Santa, a different Santa, with a giant sack of toys being pulled by a team of four horses; and riding alongside him was Krampus, carrying a switch and a basket; both of them looking merry. An old, weathered, green felt cap with fur trim and hollyberries hung from a hook on the side. Crusty reached inside the cupboard and pulled out a bottle of Nog's Menthe Rum from 1892. "We should be celebrating!"

"No, Crusty. No celebrating. No time tonight."

Crusty paused, put the bottle back and looked at his longtime friend. He dragged a small stepstool before Santa and nudged him to help him up so they stood eye-to-eye. "If I had any magic left in me," he swallowed. "I'd grant just one last wish." He patted Santa on the shoulder. "That you could remember all those letters you've answered and all those wishes you've granted, all the joy and hope and Holiday Spirit you've brought to all those children all these many years and…" He trailed off, thinking back to all his own many years, and then added, "And find happiness there."

Santa thought, and a smile slowly emerged. It was a sad smile, but for both of them, it would do. And, strangely enough, the tiredness was gone, replaced with a smoldering fierceness whose embers got stoked. "Oh, Crusty. I think there's more magic left in you than you realize. Mind the globe, old friend?"

Crusty nodded. "Turn, you whippersnapper!" Santa complied, and Crusty hopped on for a piggyback ride back into Headquarters. Crusty rocked side-to-side as Santa hobbled, rushing through the halls towards his office.

"Divvy up Feliz's list between Angel and Sirius." Santa pointed to an imaginary list that hovered in the air before him. "Have them move double-time."

Crusty looked a bit silly, the stripes of his long cap swinging to and fro as he craned his neck around Santa's to peer at the imaginary list. "Double-time, check."

"Hone in on Rumpus. If Krampus runs loose and off the handle, call all Flyers in."

"But, then…who will deliver all the toys?"

"One bridge at a time." They reached Santa's office, and Santa helped Crusty climb down. He nodded a thanks and a goodbye and as he turned away, Crusty called him back.

"Tell Krampus I said hey."

And to Santa, that was the oddest request. "He's not the Krampus you once knew, Crusty."

"And you're not the Santa he once knew. Tell him Crusty would like to share some biscuits. Over tea."

Santa twisted up his face as he rushed on, and muttered to himself, "Okay…" He marched down the hall with such force his cast cracked and crumbled off in plastery bits. He threw aside his cane and strode, determined, towards the glass doors to the outside. He pulled on his black leather boots, threw on his Santa jacket, and wrapped himself up in his thick, black leather belt. He turned to the full-length mirror and checked himself out. Those embers fully stoked, roared alive, and he looked fierce…I AM SANTA!

He turned to leave, and as the automatic doors opened and the cold wind rushed in, The Missus called him back, "Oi! Kringle!"

Santa hopped to a stop and turned. The doors shut. The fire flickered out.

"Forgetting something?" she asked.

Santa's eyes darted about, and he patted himself down—had his belt, his gloves, his boots…what could he be forgetting? Ah! Of course! he realized, and he kissed The Missus goodbye.

"I meant your hat," she smirked. She tugged the hat over his head and fixed the puff ball just so. "Where would you be without me?"

"Lost." Santa smiled.

"Hopelessly lost," she playfully jabbed him, kissing him. "Bring 'em home."

"Wish me luck."

She smiled with a wink and nudged him on, but Santa hesitated. "Keep an eye on Crusty, eh? He's a little-" He gestured with a wave of the palm…uneven.

"Go. Go," she urged him along.

## 13 – A SLIPPERY SLOPE

Elves, known for making toys, are creative types capable of making the most outrageous things imaginable. In Jack's case, in this particular moment, he was creating the most outrageous mess in Kevin's kitchen. He scoured the drawers and cabinets, pulling out things in search of what he needed. The junk drawer looked as if it had all but exploded—with dried-out pens, dull pencils, paper clips, long expired pizza coupons, rubber bands, dried-up glue sticks, and empty rolls of gift wrapping tape all thrown about across the countertops and floor. In the midst of all of his rummaging, however, he nearly missed what he was looking for when he haphazardly tossed it over his shoulder, then quickly realized what he had just thrown, and then arched backward to catch it, which of course caused him to lose his balance and fall off the stool.

He held up the roll of duct tape; the gears of his brain turning and conjuring what to make with it.

Now, it was well known that Jack and tape of any sort were not friends, as Candi would say, and duct tape was a particular nemesis, for it was particularly sticky. He carefully peeled back a corner, and then just an inch or two and thoughtfully attached it to the countertop so that he could safely unroll a long band. So far, not so bad, he thought. But when he tore the piece from the roll, the tape stuck to his hand. And when he tried to peel it off with his other hand, the ribbon began to stick to itself in one, two, and then three places. And when Jack tugged at it to get it straight again, the part sticking to the countertop unstuck itself and the tape curled on itself and Jack, and he tangled himself in it as if it were some sticky python. He tripped and fell to the floor.

"Snowballs!"

It took several attempts, and several face-plants to the floor, but Jack finally managed it…he created a sash out of duct tape that draped from his shoulder across his chest like a frighteningly inelegant Miss America, bearing Rambo-style a steak knife, a two-pronged fork, a wooden ladle, and bamboo skewers. Had he fallen just the right way, his mission would have ended fast, and in a most horrible fashion that perhaps even the Elf Nurse couldn't fix. But, he didn't fall, and still, he searched the kitchen for weapons of any sort he could add to his arsenal. A frying pan could hurt, he thought, but was too heavy and bulky, especially being of the cast iron variety. Just then, a knife block caught his attention; so much so that he didn't notice a red and green poof of light from the living room.

Santa's here.

Jack slowly drew the largest knife from the block, appreciating its possibilities. A small sword in Jack's tiny elf hands, the blade was the kind of knife you might use to carve a turkey, not realizing its purpose was to chop and dice veggies. Jack scraped it against the honing rod, imagining its use as he swung it about.

In the living room, Santa surveyed the mess, putting his palm to his head and grumbling…oi. He crunched over some smashed knickknacks, hesitating before reaching out to pet Noxen on the head. Santa knew that their embarrassingly dismal first encounter wasn't Noxen's fault—well, not any more than it might be Rudolph's fault for brightening up a foggy night with a red glow—but he still felt the sting, a smidge of despair whenever he neared the reindeer. It wasn't fair that he kept him at a distance, however understandable. Noxen greeted Santa with a brief dimming of the lights and an electric spark from his eyes, and Santa smiled his greeting in return before both of them looked about at the shambles. Christmas certainly was destroying living rooms this year. Santa's cheeks puffed out as he sighed, crunching over shattered picture frames as he made his way to the kitchen. He paused on a torn photo of Kevin and his parents—Mom and Dad's bright eyes and smiles glinted eerily between bits of glass, whereas Kevin's brooding darkness looked quite appropriate in this Christmas carnage. Santa stepped into the kitchen and watched Jack swing about the large knife, doing battle against an imaginary foe. His eyebrows furled; the rosiness of his cheeks burned through the makeup, nearly as bright as Rudolph's nose. Santa's eyes felt as heavy as his heart. "Rumpus?" he called softly.

Startled, Jack spun about, pointing the business end of the knife at Santa. He grunted, baring his teeth, his breath heaving his chest.

"Jackie?" Santa remained calm, yet cautious.

"Santa?!" Jack relaxed, recognizing the intruder. "You're here?"

Santa looked at the sharpness pointed at him. The part of him that felt like a dad to all the elves and children about the world weighed on his heart. "Of course, I'm here."

Jack looked at his knife. His teary eyes darted to the floor. "He's got Candi."

"What's with the get-up?" Santa asked, trying to lighten the moment, but Jack wasn't ready for anything light.

"It's all my fault." Jack shook his head. "He took her."

"You going to shish-kebob Krampus?"

Another nudge for lightness from Santa only brought out a viciousness from Jack the likes of which Santa hadn't ever seen. "He's got Candi!" he seethed, gripping ever tighter about the knife's handle.

Santa bit his bottom lip, weighing the moment, taking in the overwhelming hurt on Jack's face, the kind of hurt that pretends to be angry. He got down onto one knee, gentle and fatherly. "And we'll get her back," he reassured Jack, taking the knife and placing his hand on the back of Jack's shoulder. "But this isn't how we do things."

"He's evil," Jack cried. "Candi was right. He's really evil."

Santa carefully lifted the sash from Jack, appreciating its ingenuity. And it's desperation. "Wasn't always so," he said, wrapping his palm around Jack's cheek, at once trying to comfort and instruct. "And I reckon there's still a part of him that isn't so evil. But, Jackie…" Santa swallowed and sighed again. "You can't match evil for evil. That's a slipperier slope you can't fathom." Jack nodded, conceding and sorrowful. Their eyes locked until Santa's darted toward a pair of feet that poked out from behind the kitchen island. Santa rose, cocked his head aside and side-stepped to glance at Kevin's parents…collapsed in a heap. "Huh," he swallowed. "He says."

"Sleep-balls," Jack grimaced.

"I gave you that magic to fix the reindeer stampede!"

Jack frowned, and his head pulled back. "You saw that?!" To which, Santa shot his Santa Look…duh. Jack sucked through his teeth, suddenly feeling ashamed, though he didn't know why. "Is there a recommended dose? I really had to juice them up." His palm went to his eyes to massage his temples. "A few times."

"Ah," Santa sighed. "They'll feel like they've had a few too many peppermint ales." He looked about the kitchen. "When they finally wake up."

"Seriously, Santa." Jack shook his head. "Sleep-balls are the lamest superpower ever. Except maybe for Aquaman."

Santa's eyes arched, as his upper lip pulled aside from beneath his beard. "Well, thankfully, your superpower wears off come sun up." He looked about and then called up to the ceiling, "Crusty?! A little help?"

Jack looked about as well…Crusty? And then, familiar white wisps that had been called upon from a giant snow globe in Santa's office swirled in and about from the fireplace. The shattered pictures and knickknacks shimmered and rose about Noxen, who marveled and brayed and stomped as he had never seen this particular magic before, watching everything become unbroken and unfallen, finding their rightful place on the mantle and end tables that fixed themselves. The picture of Kevin and his folks righted itself on the end table, fixed so that now Mom and Dad looked picture-perfect, and Kevin was the one eerily out of place. The amount of effort the teen had put into his emphatic disinterested gloom and doom glare paid off by creating a family photo his artsy mother found striking when printed in black and white. She had even turned the photo into this year's Christmas cards sent to family and friends. Much to Kevin's dismay.

The ephemeral fog that filled in the space about Noxen tumbled and swirled into the basement, bringing sounds of the unbroken, unfallen and un-stomped as wisps swirled into the kitchen and wrapped about Jack.

"What the-?" he exclaimed, amazed as the kitchen cleaned itself. He jumped back when Kevin's parents lifted up off the floor, hovering and dead-like, with their arms drooped and their hands dragging along the floor as they floated back towards their bedroom. Jack's eyes shot wide as he stepped toward the doorway to the living room to watch them fade into the darkness of the hall. He turned back to the kitchen to see the tape, dried-out glue sticks and expired pizza coupons shoot back into the junk drawer, which slammed shut.

"Jackie Roland Rumpus!" Santa shouted, jolting Jack from his amazement. Three sleeping children, still tied to chairs, floated up from the basement and into the living room.

"I needed Krampus to find me!" Jack explained though the stern look from Santa let him know his explanation wasn't satisfactory. "It seemed like a good idea at the time!" Santa frowned and glared. "I'm…" Jack's heart ached. The children tumbled in the air, their binds untying themselves, slipping from their chairs and floating out the opening front door back to their homes and beds. "I'm so-"

"I know!" Santa snapped. "You're sorry!" He bared his teeth, shaking his head just slightly. "You're always sorry."

Jack stepped up to Santa. "But this time I'm-"

"Really sorry? Yeah, you never learn!" Santa stepped past Jack to survey the kitchen.

Jack looked up to the ceiling. "Crusty!" he called. "Make sure they're okay?!" His eyes darted about, half-expecting Crusty to materialize somewhere in the ceiling. "Krampus knocked them hard. Like, really hard." Jack turned to Santa. "Crusty can do that, right?" A shameful glare from Santa is like the most angry, admonishing look from the most angry, admonishing dad. A gust of wind blew into Jack's face and mussed his hair as the wisps swirled and rushed backward up into the fireplace…up into Crusty's fingertip that pressed against the snow globe in Santa's office.


Crusty watched the last of the wisps retreat into his fingertip, taking a curious, appreciative look at his finger. His eyes wandered about the long office, to all the books, and the piles of letters stacked and bound like old newspapers, outside to the Christmas Eve night, to the faraway mountains where Santa's telescope peered. He took an old black-felt top hat from a shelf and put it on his head, and felt a little bit like he was Santa Claus. "Time," he said, tapping against the top of the hat, "marches forward." He turned back to the ephemeral fog inside the globe.

Jack stammered, chasing after Santa—dodging the side glances and wringing his hands. Santa searched through each cabinet, slamming each door shut—seemingly harder than the previous door—as he moved on to the next cabinet.

"I'm-" Jack paused, interjecting upon himself before Santa could mock another *I'm sorry*. "I *am* sorry," he sighed. "I'm sorry I'm..." he thought a moment, accepting what everyone at The Pole had been telling him for so long. "I'm sorry I'm such a bad elf."

"Jackie!" Santa slammed shut another cabinet. "You're not a bad elf. You just do naughty things." He moved on to the next cabinet. "Nine times out of ten, given the choice between doing the naughty thing or doing the nice thing, I'd wager you'd do the nice thing." Jack's eyes grew wide, having never realized that Santa felt this way about him...really?! But Jack's elation fell flat as Santa snapped, "But in the most naughty way conceivable!"

"I-I-I don't," he stammered. "I don't think I-"

Santa finally found what he was looking for...a cylinder of salt...and he stomped towards the living room, pausing just long enough for his shoulders to tense up. His hands rose and throttled an imaginary neck in front of him. "You kidnapped three children today!"

"Five," Jack said matter-of-factly. "Technically." He grimaced. "If I'm being honest."

Santa stopped in front of the fireplace and turned back to Jack. "And who else do we know that kidnaps children on Christmas Eve?"

"It wasn't like that! I mean!" Jack thought…it was just to get Krampus to find him. It wasn't mean. It wasn't kidnapping! But, yet it was…just like Krampus! "It was just supposed to-" And then Jack realized just how much he behaved like his former idol this Christmas year. "It was just-" He tried to explain himself. To excuse himself! But as he stammered to find the words, the only two that managed their way past his lips were, "Oh! Poop!"

"Yeah," Santa nodded, bending down towards his most troublesome elf. "Poop." He sprouted back up and turned his frustration at Noxen, who nibbled at the tree.

"That's why you hate me?" Jack asked.

"Candi," Santa said. "Would you say she's bad?" Jack's face twisted up. The thought would never have occurred to him…Candi? Bad? Santa nodded, "Reckon she's been joyriding Rudolph." Jack was aghast. His eyes widened at the realization, connecting dots as Santa used his boot to clear space around the fireplace. "And I thought it was you!"

"Candi got Christmas canceled?"

"And I gather she got it uncanceled, too." He kicked away a present that had been ever so neatly wrapped in a gold foil and red bow. "You see," he said, "you just do whatever pops into your head—complete disregard for naughty or nice. She, on the other hand, considers the difference, but does the naughty thing anyway." And then he turned on Jack, shooting a look that made Jack realize something he hadn't quite ever realized before. "For you, I might add."

"For me?" Getting Christmas uncanceled, knowing how Hollyberry Farms glistened in the moonlight, sabotaging his training, the perma-swear…

Santa poured a salt line around the hearth and then closed his eyes as he turned his face up to the ceiling. "She must be the naughtiest elf ever! I can only imagine Krampus' excitement when *she* showed up. And yet, she's one of my favorites. So, Jackie." Santa turned on Jack, looking down upon him, leaning his face into Jack's, and poking Jack in the chest as he enunciated each word. "I. Don't. Hate you." He sprang up straight. "Noxen!" The reindeer turned, mid-chew, with glistening tinsel strands hanging from the side of his mouth as he munched upon a branch. An ornament that looked like a popular spongy cartoon character swung from the end of the branch. "Stop eating the tree. That can't be good for you." Santa tugged at the branch, double-checking it. "This thing even real?" Noxen gave another cautious chew before returning to the tree. Santa reached up and took the star from the treetop. He threw it down to the floor, inside the salt line, and stomped and ground it to pieces with his heel. Finally satisfied that the star bits were fine enough, he clapped, turned to the fireplace and sized it up. "Now. Candi."

He closed his eyes, turned his palms out, and calmly uttered, "Krampusnacht."

Jack climbed onto the end table and sat, waiting for something more than nothing. But nothing happened. Santa remained still, palms out, eyes closed. The fireplace stayed cold and dark. Jack glanced back and forth between the two. "Tried that," he finally said.

"Shush, you." Santa shook an annoyed hand at him. "There's more to it," he insisted. "Been a while."

"Bu-"

And now two annoyed hands shook at Jack. "Bu-buh-buh-buh-buh…hush. I'm thinking." Jack bit his bottom lip as if to keep the rest of his words trapped inside. And Santa thought. "Krampusnacht steht vor der Tür," he began at last, his eyes growing cloudy and gray. "Mit Rute und Korb. Krampusnacht steht vor der Tür." He trailed off, lips quivering as if to start a word but being cautious that the right word was being started. And, finally confident he had found the words deep in the nooks and crannies of his mind, his eyes grew wide, and he pointed at the fireplace. "Böse Kinder fürchten ihn."

Impatience swung Jack's legs about. "All that just to open a door?"

"Hush, you." Popcorn flashes bounced about Santa, who hopped back as the fireplace roared to life.

The heat and glare made Jack pull back, excitement glistening on his rosy cheeks, flames reflecting in his eyes. "What are we gonna do?"

Santa pointed into the fire. "I am going to go in there and get Candi." And then he pointed to the end table. "You are going to stay with Noxen."

"What?!" Jack protested, hopping to his feet. "No! I want to help!" His fists clenched in front of his chest as he dramatically emphasized, "I *need* to help!"

"Too dangerous, Jackie. Once I go in, Polar Magic will be useless."

"Which is a roundabout way of saying you really, really need me."

"Jackie, no. I can't do what I need to do and worry about you, too." Jack, of course, started to protest even more, but Santa cut him off with a pointed finger. "Promise me. Stay with Noxen."

"Okay," Jack caved, but not before crossing his fingers behind his back.

And from The Santa Look came, "I mean it, Jackie."

"Uh-huh," he nodded.

Frustrated, Santa grabbed Jack's arm and shook it to show he wasn't fooled. "No more games, Rumpus!"

"Fine," he sighed, pouting. "I'll stay with Noxen."

Although doubtful, Santa cautiously turned back to the fireplace. "Wish me luck." A red and green aura shimmered as he stepped over the salt and into the flames.

"Santa?" Jack cocked his head askew. How strange it was to see Santa bent in the flames, yet not burning as he looked back at Jack. "Thought your leg was broken."

Santa feigned surprise. "It's a Christmas miracle!" He touched his finger to his nose, nodded with a wink, and vanished.

Jack stared into the fire. "Good luck." He thought he could see the shadow of Santa darting about somewhere behind the flames. With an unbroken leg. Candi was perhaps the naughtiest elf ever? For him, no less? And he was as wrong about Santa hating him as everyone else was wrong about Jack hating Santa. This night wasn't supposed to go like this, he thought, and yet the more he thought on it, losing himself to the flickering light, he suspected it couldn't have gone any other way.

## 14 - MAKE LIKE AN ELF

The Naughty children had accepted their fate. Crying was useless. Screaming was hollow. They were in Hell, on Christmas Eve no less. Nobody was going to help them. Candi and Kevin, on the other hand, were furious with sweat—climbing the bars, tugging on the bars, shaking the bars, and occasionally throttling the bars as if choking the life out of the demon who dragged them there—looking for any kind of weakness. Kevin had lent her his socks to wear on her hands to protect them from getting zapped. The red-striped sport socks ran all the way up her arms to her shoulders and reeked like a sweaty teen, which initially made her nauseated. Determined to break free, however, Candi pushed through, but they weren't going anywhere any time soon. For that wasn't how Krampus operated his Christmas Eve.

Kevin turned to the other kids. "C'mon!" he urged. "Help us!"

Sullen eyes looked back at him with hardly a movement. Just then, the strangest thing happened. Candi stopped testing the bars. She let go, slapping her stinky-sock-covered hands over her pointy ears as she fell to the ground. She winced in pain and her eyes twitched, searching for the source of a most painful noise. An eight-year-old girl stood in the center of the cave. Her long blond hair hid her face, but it was obvious that, unlike the other kids, her tears weren't silent. She sobbed. She howled. And, well, she cried the kind of tantrum cry an eight-year-old might cry upon finding herself locked in a cave in Hell. On Christmas Eve. Her name was Amy, the girl whose stocking belonged to Feliz's missing Naughty List.

"Oh, please don't cry," Candi pleaded, approaching Amy like one might a cornered badger—with extreme caution and perhaps wondering why you might be approaching such a mongrel in the first place. Still, she tried to comfort the girl, touching her forearm. "Crying kids is like the worst sound to an elf." Amy's cries escalated, as did Candi's wincing…unlike her attempt at comforting, which all but abated. "Seriously, kid! Nails on a chalkboard." A few of the other Naughty kids shuddered at the thought, though it was apparent most had never heard the shrill noise that sent shivers up one's arms and down their spine. Were chalkboards no longer a thing, Candi wondered, but only briefly, as she looked about…what to do, what to do? "Gah!" she gasped at another loud outburst from Amy. Her hands slapped back over her ears, the pain knocking her off her feet. "I know!" She rushed to the bars and spied a broken doll. "Kevin? Can you reach that?"

Kevin knelt and stretched his arms through the bars, fingers reaching, further, and further, as if he could will them to grow or perhaps pull his shoulder right from its socket. But, just as he was about to reach the broken plaything, he pulled back and looked at Candi. "Wait a minute! Why's she crying?"

"I want my mommy!" the girl shrieked as if the answer to his question should be obvious, causing Candi to double over on the ground as if kicked in the gut.

"But *how* is she crying? And why can I talk?" Silently crying Naughty kids all looked to Kevin.

"Doll first," Candi winced. "Please?" As soon as Kevin had the doll, Candi snatched it and gave it to Amy, with a not-so-comforting pleading grin of desperation. Amy hugged the doll, sniffled and quieted, and Candi's shoulders drooped as she began to relax. But then Amy took a look at the doll—its broken arm, singed hair and burnt dress, missing an eye and covered in dirt and soot. She threw it down, horrified, as if the doll were the corpse of her most favorite imaginary friend.

"It don't even have a eye!" she shouted, crying again.

"O. M. G!" Candi snapped, covering her ears again. "I really am in Hell." She panicked, eyes frantically looking about for something else to try, her insides shuddering in pain from the noise, when she spied the return of Krampus' shadow-ball. It descended and hovered in front of the cave before entering, mesmerizing everyone as it seeped through the bars and breaking apart like a hand of swirling, menacing fingers. As it headed for Amy, the girl remembered what Candi had done when they first heard the word *dunkelstimma*, and she quickly slapped her hands over her mouth. Still, a dark magic jerked Amy as shadowy wisps emerged, oozing between her fingers before launching, dissipating, and swirling into the shadow ball. Though still crying, Amy fell silent once again.

"That didn't happen with me," Kevin observed.

"Well," Candi thought. "The silence is…better?"

Kevin looked at Amy, and then about to the other terrified Naughty kids. "Imagine screaming for help, but you can't make a sound."

And suddenly Candi felt awful, despite Amy subjecting her to one of the worst sounds to an elf. "Oh," she said, simply, touching Amy's forearm with as much comfort as she could muster.

"Maybe Hell will do you good," Kevin frowned as he remembered. "Raging silence takes them home."

"What's that?" Candi asked.

"What Krampus said. Raging silence takes them home."

"Speaking of which…" Candi nodded, and they returned to the furious task of searching the bars for any weaknesses. And again, they kicked, and they tugged, and they sweat, and they throttled for a time. After one particular throttling, Kevin cried out a primal grunt through gritted teeth and gave the bars a kick and a punch, hardly reacting to the pain in his knuckles. Candi had climbed to the top, looking for loose connections between the bars and the cave wall. She paused on his grunt and slid down to meet him at eye level. Something was bothering him, she thought, beyond the obvious problems they faced. He palmed his sweaty hair out of his face, catching his breath, and looking to Candi's eyes. "Krampus didn't want Emily, Stephen, or Micha. Why me? Or Ash? She wasn't even a part of the block party."

"Who knows why he does what he does?" she shrugged.

"But...I'm the only kid who can talk here. Why just me?"

"Because I slapped your mouth shut?"

Kevin nodded towards Amy, who listed silently in the center of the cave. Tears streaked the soot on her cheeks. "Didn't work on her," he said, giving the bars another shake and another angry grunt. He turned his back to the bar and slid down as his resolve diminished. "It's hopeless. I must belong here."

Candi watched him slide down, frowning. "Don't say that!" She slid down to him. "It's never hopeless. Jackie thought he belonged here, too. But he was wrong. And you're wrong. Unless..." She turned about, towards all the hopeless faces of the silent Naughty kids. "Unless you're right. And you really do belong here."

"Gee, thanks." He bugged his eyes out to the space in front of him.

"No, I mean..." She grew excited. "What if that's the point? You *don't* belong here because you realize that you *do* belong here." It wasn't quite The Santa Look that he shot at her, but it was a look of confusion as if he couldn't process what seemed so incredibly stupid to him. Candi understood the look, having given one similar to Jack on countless occasions. "It's about penance," she explained. "Remorse. And you must be feeling guilty about something." She turned to Amy, pointing. "And you! What if you're an ungrateful brat?" Amy's eyes grew wide, distraught. "No! No!" Candi insisted, rushing over to pat Amy on the hand. "I'm not saying you are…but what if that's why you're here? You got your voice back, but then rejected the doll because she doesn't have an eye? And then poof!" She looked about the Naughty kids, who all looked thoughtful back at her. "What would all of you do differently so Krampus wouldn't bring you here?" And as they all reflected, wisps of dark shot back into the cell and into the children's mouths. The wisps hit them in the back of their throats, jostling their newly-enlightened minds backward. They all gasped when their voices hit them. "See that, Kevin! It's never hopeless." She smiled, slapping him on his knee. "Now make like an elf and help me?" He briefly considered his smelly sock, dangling over the edge of her outstretched hand, before smiling and reaching back.

Just then, Santa peered from around the side. And Santa, not knowing that Candi had already fixed one of the next problems on his to-do list when helping the Naughty kids find their voices, lost all element of surprise as the children charged the bars calling out "Santa!" Such happiness and joy! "Santa!" For this year he wasn't just the jolly old elf to bring them presents…he was their savior. "Santa!" Oi, he thought, urging and pleading for them to quiet.

Somewhere high up above, at the end of a dusty cliff path, burned a fire from the wrong side of a fireplace…Kevin's fireplace. And in Kevin's living room, Jack paced about as Noxen feasted upon the tree. Were Jack like any other elf, say, Mickie, being told by Santa to stay put and to do nothing would have found Jack staying put and doing exactly nothing until he was told to do something otherwise. But, as we know, Jack wasn't like all the other elves. His impatience grew as wild as his imagination…wondering what could be happening to Candi…the guilt weighing upon him that it was all his fault…that he made this stupid wish year after year…that- "Gah!" How his thoughts swirled upon themselves! He stomped off to the kitchen.

And Noxen, who had been minding his own business and munching on the Christmas tree, stopped mid-chew, turning a thoughtful gaze towards Jack's departure. His antler brushed through the edges of the branches, knocking a few ornaments from their hooks. More tinsel strands hung from the sides of his mouth, glistening with the firelight. When Jack returned, determined, gripping the knife and wearing his weapon-sash, Noxen protested. He grunted and stomped his foot.

"I know what Santa said," Jack insisted, stepping around the reindeer. "But-"

More grunts came from the beast, along with a fierce red glow.

"How is doing a nice thing naughty?" Jack charged into the flames, and Noxen bowed down after him, biting onto the sash and yanking him back such that Jack slammed his head into the firebox ceiling, tangled in the tape, feet kicking, until the tape finally tore and he tumbled to the ashes and burning embers. Jack seethed, on all fours…the only heat he felt was his rage until he spied something sparkling in the ashes. He reached for it, almost hypnotic. "Huh…he says." He crawled back out of the flames, standing up to show Noxen. "Candi's necklace."

A jack-o-lantern bat made festive with a Santa hat.

"I made her this." Noxen's eyes shimmered. Jack thought back, swallowing as his heart grew heavy. "Right after I failed getting my Wrapping Badge. My last chance." He looked into Noxen's silvery eyes. "Too many failed badges. Got kicked out of the Elf Brigade." He sniffled. "I acted like I didn't care, but Candi knew. I just wanted to belong to something. Anything. Who needs the Elf Brigade, she said." His misty eyes were lost to the memory. "We'll be our own brigade. Just us. The Jolly Dead Brigade! I made her this. And she gave me-," Jack held up the candy-striped ring that only fit the middle finger of his right hand. "Oh!" he said, quickly retreating his hand as he realized he was giving Noxen the bird. "She's everything good about The Pole, Noxen. Everything good to me, anyway. I have to get her back."

A grunt. A brief, red glow, and Jack got the message.

"For a freak with tinsel hanging out of his mouth, you're pretty sharp." Jack tugged the tinsel free, a little disgusted as the strands slipped out from the back of Noxen's throat. He scratched his muzzle and smiled. "I need to be more of a freak like you. Minus the tinsel. And you…" He hung a red ornament on the end of an antler and watched the flames flicker in its swaying reflection. "Maybe you can be more of a freak like me. I can keep my promise if you'll stay with me." A dim shimmer of appreciation. Jack watched the ornament swing. "But I do need something."

# 15 - BATTLE!

Krampus' house looked out of place in Hell; a traditional German cottage, with ornate woodwork and trim, fairy-tale-like shutters, and wood shingles. So terribly out of place. Quaint, cozy, warm and inviting. It just didn't belong. The flower boxes hanging outside the windows long-held nothing but barren dirt, which the trolls dutifully cleared of cobwebs, for even weeds didn't grow in them. Long-dead trees flanked the house, such that if imagined just right, one could picture this home in some ancient forest. The flagstone path winded through the dead trees and was swept clean by the trolls, who all seemed happy to serve their Krampus. And it wasn't just the path and the flowerboxes that needed tending, for in Hell, soot was a constant nemesis. Trolls washed the windows, swept the chimney, mopped the roof, and when the day finished, a new team would arrive to start the cleaning all over yet again.

Since soot made its way inside as well, the cleaning didn't end at the front door. The inside of the cottage remained constantly busy with the hustle and bustle of the house trolls, who dusted, wiped, scrubbed and swept endlessly. All happy to serve. Aside from trolls, and ceaseless soot, being in Hell, and well, having a

Christmas demon for an owner, the cottage was otherwise homey and inviting. Mahogany walls that could not decide between being a deep, rich red or brown, were a canvas of blooming flower patterns—painstakingly painted, not printed, mind you, as was the custom in the old days. The couch and chairs and tables were all carved in the finest detail, including the cupboard which looked suspiciously like the cupboard in Crusty's cottage—a hand-carved winter scene of Krampus and Santa cheerily heading forth—together—some Christmas Eve long ago. But, whereas Crusty's cupboard held an ancient cap off its side, Krampus' displayed an old photo, hung just slightly askew. A house troll flittered by with a feather duster and flicked away its dust, righting it before moving on to some other dusty thing. It was an ancient photo; the colors had been painted in over the black-and-white print. But what photo might hold Krampus' attention seemed even odder—like some family portrait, thirteen men peered back. Some smiled, others pouted. Some were tall, and others quite short. Fat and skinny. Festive and frightening. Clearly related to one another, brothers perhaps, though a few of them looked rather trollish with their bulbous noses and thick hands.

Krampus nestled into his favorite red velvet chair, looking outside at the rocky, barren view, sipping a dainty cup of tea, pinky-out. And when he heard a far-off cry, his eyes turned aside. He beamed a huge smile at the troll serving him tea. "They're here, troll," he said, just as a dark sinister cloud brooded about his face. His voice deepened and grew gravelly. "I'm going Christmas shopping."

That far-off cry belonged to Jack, who charged along the narrow path on Noxen. He screamed another war cry, waving about a meat tenderizer that looked like a club in his hands. A new tape sash carried brightly-colored ball ornaments, bouncing as he galloped along. His Santa sack, tied around his neck, whipped about like a long cape.

And Krampus wasn't the only one to hear Jack's cry. Santa moved quickly, using a rock and a stick to pry out one of the hinge pins from the gate—his white gloves protecting him from the shocking spell. He stopped working upon hearing Jack, closed his eyes and sighed in frustration. "Rumpus," he grumbled, rushing back to work. "We must hurry. Candi, tell him I don't want any help-" But just as the pin finally fell, Krampus tackled Santa from the side—a dark blur whooshing past as he and Santa disappeared.

Candi neared the bars as close as she dared, eyes darting side-to-side. "Santa?" But Santa was gone. She looked down, way down below, to where trolls emerged from a cave and stomped up the path. "Snowballs," she gasped. Across the way, near a bridge of rocky pillars, Krampus let go of Santa, tumbling him into a pile of lost toys. Santa winced, arching his back, reaching under and pulling out the remnants of an old wooden train. His eyes widened, seeing Krampus bounding toward him for another tackle and he did the only thing he could think of. He beaned Krampus in the head with the train, admittedly not the most skillful defense, but desperate times, desperate measures.

And the lack of skill wasn't missed on Krampus, who stopped, stunned. "Ow!" He rubbed where the train cracked against him. "Really?"

Santa hopped to his feet, and they began circling one another. Under normal circumstances, Santa might have a witty comeback, perhaps something about the crazy train finally reaching its destination. But Santa was tired and crabby and not in the mood for jokes. Plus, as often as he and Krampus had butted heads over the years, he had never seen Krampus so off-kilter. "This isn't us, Krampus!" He cautiously reached for a long, thick dead branch.

"And what do you know about *us*, Kringle?"

"We used to ride together."

"Before you stole Christmas!" Krampus lunged, charging at Santa, and just as he reached him, Santa jabbed the stick. Right into his belly. Krampus heaved as the wind knocked out of him, and his momentum launched him upward and over Santa, crashing down and rolling back to his feet. Krampus bared his teeth, flashing his long tongue with a howl. Santa shrieked and fled, hearing another one of Jack's war cries getting close.

But it wasn't actually a war cry that Santa had heard, but rather Jack's fearful shriek. As Noxen charged around a sharp bend, the reindeer's footing missed and they slid over the cliff's edge. And in a moment of panic, Jack forgot...Noxen flies! The reindeer continued on his turn through the air, eyes burning bright, casting a shadow on the face of the cliff that looked suspiciously like a child pretending to be a rock, yet failing horribly. "Down, Noxen!" They dove to where Ash dangled motionless out of fear of loosening the tree. "Ashanti Omondi?" He quickly swooped her up, with Mhambi flailing about behind her, still tangled in the blanket. She barely had time to register she had been rescued when she noticed they were headed back up.

"Jack?! I need to go down!"

"I need to go up!"

"Down," she cried, unaware that Noxen was the cause of her newfound melancholy, and instead blaming it on Jack ignoring her need to descend. And when Jack ignored her, she climbed up onto Noxen's back and hopped onto one of his antlers. The reindeer brayed and twisted, trying to get her off his head, spiraling down. Jack fought for control but failed. Each time he pulled up only caused more confusion for Noxen, who now tumbled through the air such that Ash fell off. At last, he got control and dove again for Ash, catching each other's hand.

"I have to get to the cottage," she pleaded, looking down, the rush of air spraying her tears off the sides of her face. She wasn't all that high anymore, but the dread she felt made the ground seem impossibly out of reach.

"And I have to rescue Candi. And Santa. And the Naughty kids."

"Jack!" she looked up to him. "You have to let me go!" She looked down to the dirty rocks zipping below her dangling feet.

"Santa wouldn't-"

"It's all I want for Christmas!" she cried.

Jack gasped. Her one Christmas wish! How Santa must have felt all those years ignoring Jack's one Christmas wish. Perhaps the old elf really did know better. But Jack knew—just knew—that if he didn't grant Ash her one wish, she would find a way to make it happen anyway. Just as Jack would. Or did, rather. He felt so torn.

"Jack…please!"

Noxen grunted, frustrated, protesting against what Jack was considering. "I'm sorry," he finally said.

"But-" Ash began, misunderstanding the apology. Jack was truly sorry for granting her that wish. He let go, and her eyes widened with grateful surprise as she began to fall. "Thank you!" Her arms and legs flailed about as she twisted herself in the air like some falling cat.

"I'll find you!" he promised, hoping it was one of those promises he could keep. Ash landed with a roll, popped up and shook off the dirt before disappearing into the remains of a once-thriving forest.

Noxen brayed. "I know! Santa's going to kill me." They coasted along for a bit. "Nobody wants my help today. I just don't know what to do here." The reindeer grunted. "Right!" And with that, they shot up and galloped back onto the path. They rushed down the last stretch toward the jail, leaping over toys, logs, and boulders, to round a corner into a hard stop in front of a troll that guarded the jail now that Santa was here. Jack flipped over Noxen's antlers and landed a foot-kick to the troll's chest.

"Jackie!" Candi grinned.

The troll scrambled to his feet and rushed Jack, who shouted "Water bomb!" before ripping one of the ornaments from his sash and fast-balling it at the troll. It shattered against the bewildered troll's head, drenching his face with water. The troll shook its head as Jack observed, rather disappointed, "Well, that was kinda…lame." He lobbed a second ornament at the troll, shouting "Flour bomb!" Poof! The troll now coughed through white dust, wiping a pasty, sticky mess from its eyes, growling.

"How's that supposed to help?" Candi asked. "You're just making him angry."

"Distraction," Jack beamed, nodding back. "Noxen!" Noxen snorted, charging and scooping the troll with his antlers, racing away with the troll waving its arms and legs in protest, passing Krampus and Santa at the pillar bridge. Had Santa a moment to think, he might have thought to call over Noxen to help him escape. But he didn't think. And he didn't call. And he was out of room to run with Krampus on his tail. He paused at the edge of a deep crevice; tiny rocks skittering underneath his feet into the dark below. He turned back to Krampus, swallowed a glance down into the deep, and then leaped over to the first jagged rocky pillar. His leap fell short, however. He tossed his stick just in time to free his hands so that he could grip the pillar's edge, and he hung as the stick rolled across the surface, nearly twisting off the other side. Krampus reached the crevice and skidded to a halt, grinning and enjoying the sight of Santa hanging.

Santa glared over his shoulder, grunting and groaning as he climbed. "Steal Christmas?" Santa asked at last. "Ha!" He climbed a little more, his boot loosening rocks as he stretched and pushed, feeling less and less a little too-oldy as he had of late. "Steal from who? You?"

"It was ours," Krampus sniveled.

Santa pulled his knee up onto the pillar and pulled up, bent over and huffing as he caught his breath. Finally, he straightened, the thought of Krampus' complaint coming clear, and in his most you're-an-idiot tone he could muster (his tone sounding suspiciously like Jack's) he semi-chuckled, semi-feigned surprise. "No, it wasn't." Krampus groaned and leapt. Santa spun about, swiping the stick and swinging like he was aiming for a home run. The branch whacked Krampus hard in the chest and split in two. Krampus flipped back, landing with a thud.

Way down below, after Ash had landed and rolled into the dead forest, she found a place to hide and take a moment to inspect Mhambi. Her robot spider was in bad shape. Bent legs, broken legs, and missing legs. Even though she knew that Mhambi couldn't feel pain or even sadness for the sad state it was in, Mhambi's wounds wounded Ash. "You sure are a fright," she groaned. "Can you retract your legs?" She winced, watching Mhambi comply. The two remaining good legs folded up neatly into the side, but the two remaining broken ones merely twitched—one of them popping at the knee so that the lower part of the leg dangled and wobbled from a wire that eventually gave out. The slender bit of metal landed at Ash's feet, along with Ash's optimism. She reached into a vest pocket for a screwdriver, only to find a used and crusty tissue. "Ugh!" she groaned, patting down her other pockets. "This night!" She looked about on the dirt and then back into the distance where she had originally fallen. The screwdriver must have fallen out, as lost as all the weird and random toys this place had collected over the years. "This adventure certainly isn't going as planned." She thought for a quick moment and apologized to the robot for what she was about to do, and then admonished herself for forgetting Mhambi wouldn't care. Couldn't care. It just wasn't part of her programming! She snapped off the broken legs and stowed them in her vest—zipping shut the pocket and pressing down the Velcro for good measure—and then she hooked the two good legs through a utility hoop on the vest. She double-checked its battery levels. "Just keep recording until you run out of juice, okay?" Her broken spider chirped. "Once I get Maia charged up, I'll give you a boost."

She looked hundreds of feet up the rocky cliffs, towards the sounds of battle, hoping Jack would know she lied to him…that she didn't have just one Christmas wish. As much as she needed to find Maia, she so desperately wished to not get stuck in this place.

Up by Krampus' jail, Noxen guarded the troll, who was bound and struggling at the reindeer's feet, wriggling like some maggot that had lost its way. Jack used the hinge pin and meat tenderizer to tap out the second pin, wincing at the occasional zaps he received whenever he accidentally brushed the metal with his bare skin. Once the pin finally fell, Kevin kicked down the gate. Candi ran to Jack, wrapping herself around the surprised elf and kissing him. "Hope!" she beamed.

"Hope?" Jack twisted his face, confused. "What?"

Candi turned back to Kevin, pointing to him for emphasis. "There's always hope."

Now standing a little too close to Noxen, Kevin collapsed in a fit of despair, sobbing as if his very soul were being sucked from him and he waffled between clinging to it or embracing the relief it might give him should he simply let it go from him.

"Kevin?" Candi worried, putting her arms on his shoulders before realizing. "Noxen!"

Noxen turned, eyes shimmering, edging closer to the distraught teen, and bowing to him. Kevin looked past him to where Santa and Krampus battled on the rock pillars, hopelessness consuming him.

"It's Noxen," Candi huffed. "He absorbs light and energy around him. It's dreadful if the dark is all you see." She took Kevin's hand and put it to Noxen's snout. "Look past the dark. See him for all he is. The good. The light…" She turned to the Naughty kids, speaking louder. "He's a teddy bear!"

"A moody one," Jack added. "But still."

"He's all love!" Candi promised as Kevin swallowed and shook off the dread, calming and catching his breath.

"Santa," Kevin exhaled, pointing past the elves, nodding towards Santa and Krampus. As Santa readied to leap to the next pillar, Krampus stomped his cloven hoof and a powerful blast radiated out. The pillar crumbled and shifted, tilting as cracked stones large and small tumbled down and bounced against the rock wall. Santa rocked back and forth to keep his bearings, and then finally used the pillar's falling momentum to jump over to the next pillar, only to find Krampus already standing before him.

Readying for a rescue, Jack started to hop onto Noxen, but Candi yanked him back. "Santa. He said don't help him."

"But-" Jack started to protest, pushing forward.

Candi gripped his forearm, adamant. "Given the choice between Santa or the children, who do you think he'd want you to help?" Jack grunted, pacing, tangled in his conflicting thoughts. He couldn't just leave Santa here. He watched Krampus and Santa circling one another.

As Santa's foot scuttled near the rock's edge, he glanced far below. Having flown his sleigh all these years, Santa wasn't ever afraid of heights. It was falling that frightened him. Definitely falling. He took a cautious step away from the edge, towards his enemy. "Christmas is bigger than either one of us, Krampus."

"You reward the Nice kids. I punish the Naughty ones. It's not any bigger than that."

Santa leapt to the other side of the crevice and turned back. "Oh, Krampus…"

"But you went and took all the glory. Stopped bringing me along. Replaced me for lumps of coal. What kind of punishment is that?" Krampus vaulted, punching Santa and knocking him onto his back. Santa saw a small band of flying reingoyles darting for Jack, and he knew he had to keep Krampus occupied until the children were safe. He scrawled away backward, grasping for any random lost toy he could find and pitching them at Krampus.

Down deep in the dead forest, Ash sprinted towards Krampus' cottage. She would occasionally glance at the commotion above…unable to see the details, but hearing the shouts and battle cries, seeing the swarms of flying creatures darting about and appearing at times as one, like a murmuration of starlings sweeping across this hellish sky. Lower, trolls scampered everywhere as they made their way up the various winding paths. All of this commotion seemed singular in its intent to stop Santa and keep the Naughty kids, but their efforts all seemed a rather chaotic and disorganized anger. Ash imagined they were so bent in their mission for no other reason than Krampus had simply told them to be so.

Her path led to a small clearing, a wide patch of dirt where several other paths crisscrossed in differing directions. And as she bounded towards that clearing, she caught sight of something that moved slow and graceful, completely disregarding the mission that otherwise seemed to have consumed every other creature in this forsaken place. The shock of the encounter caused Ash to trip upon herself, and she fell to the ground just before the clearing. She face-planted into the dirt, but didn't cry out for fear of the large skeletal horse hearing her. She scooched backward behind a tree and peered around.

The skeleton horse grazed slow and deliberate as if it didn't realize it was dead and imagined itself eating lush grass that perhaps once grew in the clearing. Its translucent skin had rotted away and draped over its frame like a ratty, thin veil that wafted in the hot wind that blew only as one of its other imagined things. Contrary to this dark and dead, yet undead, creature was the wreath of bright and colorful flowers and ribbons that decorated its head. "Mari Lwyd!" Ash gasped, rather accidentally, and rather out loud.

The horse quickly jerked its head in Ash's direction as Ash slapped her hand over her mouth. Tiny bells on the ends of its ribbons rattled. Ash had stumbled across Mari Lwyd and many other dark monsters while researching Krampus. She had never imagined the horse was real—as usually, it was just festive men who paraded around a hobby horse made with a dead horse's skull. This horse's skull, again although dead, seemed eerily alive as it twisted slowly towards Ash, though looking about as if double-checking if it had really heard its name being called, or perhaps just experienced another imagined thing. And seemingly sure someone was afoot, it hissed an eerie wind-like howl that sent chills down Ash's spine. Her hands went from her mouth to her ears as Mhambi chirped in protest. "Shh…" she pleaded as quietly as she could muster.

The creature turned its head aside and began to sing in a weirdly, hauntingly, yet angelic voice.

> *"I am home without a home.*
> *In this strange land I roam.*
> *Hungry and lost, yet full and free*
> *Surely I'm known, but who might you be?"*

Ash closed her eyes, wishing the beast away. Mhambi ignored her pleas for quiet. "Surely I'm known!" the horse sang again, though this time with a touch of fury. Its legs galloped at a fierce speed, its back and head undulating in time. Its thin skin and ribbons fluttered behind her, yet for all the racing, Mari Lwyd hovered quite slowly towards Ash's hiding spot. "Who might you be?"

"She demands a song," Ash surmised. In the versions of the custom she had read about, the men would sing riddles and insults at a homeowner who would then sing riddles and insults back. If the men were outwitted, they would move on to another house. If the homeowner lost, however, the men were permitted entry for a pint of ale. Christmas is an even weirder holiday than I imagined, Ash thought, looking about for a direction to flee that would get her closer to Maia. But what happens when it isn't just festive men looking for free beer, she wondered.

"Who. Might. You. Be!?" the horse demanded in song, stepping ever closer.

"Forgive me!" Ash stepped out from behind her tree. "I don't sing." Her eyes darted here and there for an escape as her voice faked her apology. "And I-I don't have any ale."

Mari Lwyd pushed forward, bumping Ash into the bark of the barren tree, holding her there with her bony snout. A hot and misty breath puffed from the hollow holes where its nose once was. The fluttering of its ghostly skin whipped behind her in her sudden jerk toward Ash. Ash swallowed her fear, knowing she'd have to sing her response if she wanted to live. But even on a good day, without the threat of death from a ghostly horse, in the depths of Hell, Ash wouldn't sing. She had even gotten in trouble in music class one year as the teacher insisted the middle school kids would hold a holiday concert. While leading the class through a hearty rendition of Jingle Bells, the music teacher suddenly slammed her fists against the piano keys and demanded from Ash, "Why aren't you singing!?"

Ash looked back at the staring eyes that all surrounded her, and responded quite simply, without any defiance or disrespect, "Because I don't want to." She was sent to the principal's office, given a week of detention, and was assigned a volunteer job at the concert in lieu of a non-singing performance. She doubted Mari Lwyd would accept that Ash simply didn't want to sing. The bony snout thumped her into the tree again. "Oh!" she gasped, her breath slipping away from her. "I'm Ashanti Omon-" Another bony thump pinned her against the tree, as Ash reactively, and rather quite awkwardly, broke into a rap.

> *"DEE! from Algonquin, Illinois*
> *And I hope to not offend with a rap instead of song.*
> *But something's wrong.*
> *I'm here to make right*
> *Krampus has a friend is why I'm here tonight…"*

Her voice trailed off, overwhelmed by her own awkwardness, as she realized that, even though she was more willing to rap than sing, she couldn't rap well either. Her voice held tight in her throat as she flinched with another long sigh of hot, ghostly breath escaping the horse. Ash added a couple of desperate beat-boxing sounds with matching head bobs as she watched the specter step backward a few paces and then lower itself on its front legs, bowing its permission for Ash's passage. "Oh!" she gasped again, practically peeling herself from the bark and racing past the creature to the far side of the clearing. She had hoped the skeletal horse wouldn't be offended at her quick departure, and to be sure, she stopped just where the path to Krampus' cottage picked up again and she turned back. "Thank you!" she called back and then thought a moment. "I mean," she added in a sing-songy tone. "Thank you!" She shook off the shudder of hearing herself sing and sprinted deeper into the dead forest, on the lookout now for any other holiday monster that might surprise her.

At Krampus' jail, Jack and Candi urged the Naughty kids on and into the Santa sack. One by one they climbed inside, shocked at the endless red interior. "All the way to the back," Candi shouted, trying to keep the opening clear…but there was no back! The sack seemed to go on forever and ever. As Jack nudged Randy Jones, he was in such a hurry that he didn't even give pause, thinking he might have recognized him from somewhere. When a reingoyle swooped down and then sprang up from the cliff's edge, surprising them, Jack reacted on instinct. He dropped his hold on the sack and swung at the beast with the meat tenderizer…knocking it out of the air and sending it tumbling down in a single blow. Jack gasped at what he had done, wide-eyed. "Don't." He watched the animal tumble down into the dark. "Oh! Don't tell Santa about that."

Kevin pointed to where Krampus knelt over Santa. "I don't think he'll care."

"Kevin, help Candi." Jack shoved his end of the sack opening to Kevin. "I've gotta-"

"Jackie, no!" Candi insisted. "Santa said no."

"Take Noxen," he ordered, bounding away towards Santa, who scrounged around for a Magic 8 Ball.

The fingers of Santa's once-white gloves stretched and bent and clawed across the rock, but the ball remained slightly out of reach. "It was one thing to punish them with a switch and a rod," Santa snapped. "But then you started dragging them here!"

Krampus frowned. "They need to learn their lesson!"

"By stealing their voices? What you do isn't teaching." He still couldn't get his fingers around the 8 Ball. "It's torture. And I want no part in it. That's why we stopped riding together."

"So the Naughty List keeps growing."

"And now you're coming after my own with Rumpus and Candi? That crosses a new line."

"What do you care what Krampus does?"

Santa gave up on the Magic 8 Ball, and instead, he threw a powerful punch to Krampus' face and rolled over so that he now knelt over Krampus. "Because I'm Santa Claus," he snapped. And in a determined and furious, yet not-so-Santa-y moment, he spat, "Dammit!"

Krampus gave a slight nod as if letting Santa in on a tiny secret. "Not for much longer." He kicked up, launching Santa up and over his head and over the cliff.

Santa fell, tumbling through the air. "Oh…ho…ho…" Yes, falling was Santa's greatest fear.

Candi's cry at seeing him fall had yanked Krampus' attention, just as Jack reached the first pillar, skidding to a halt and watching Santa tumble into the deep. "Santa!" he cried out, as a swarm of reingoyles and gargoyles rose.

Krampus pointed towards the Naughty kids. "Hurry, trolls! Keep the children!" As he charged towards Jack, easily moving from one pillar to the next, Jack's attention volleyed between him and Santa. And just as Krampus grabbed for Jack, Jack did the only thing that made sense to him. He jumped. Right over the cliff. "Fool!" Krampus shot, watching Jack fall a moment before bounding away towards Candi.

It was a good thing for Ash that Krampus had called everyone into battle, for when she finally reached Krampus' cottage amid a dead forest, no one was there. No gargoyles guarding. No trolls sweeping soot. Ash crept from the tree line to the cottage and peered in the window to see if anyone was home. Aside from being out of place, the inside looked much like any other old home. And this one was empty.

She snuck around to the side of the house to where a sorta-garden sorta-grew. It was tended well enough, with prickly fruits on thick vines twisting about themselves in neat rows that burst with autumn colors—orange, yellow, brown and black—and a deep crimson threading itself through the patch. Certainly, nothing Ash dared to taste a bite of. At the end of the crimson thread, resting above this patch upon a post was Maia, being used as a decorative garden gazing ball. Ash rushed to it and scooped it up like a lost puppy. "Maia!"

The sphere returned the greeting with a faint chirp and a brief red glow that took from her the very last bits of life from her battery. Ash inspected the few scratches and dings along its surface as she dug through a pocket for a cord. She plugged one end into a recharge pack, and the other end into Maia's port. "Hopefully, this is all you need." She turned it about again, but didn't see any further damage.

"Okay, then." She looked up to the battle overhead. "How do we get back up to that mess?" She would likely be found if she took any of the paths the trolls had taken. She decided it would be best to probably hurry back to where Jack had dropped her and hopefully, he would get back to her. She darted towards the path, but from around the corner of the cottage, a giant creature jumped into her path.

"What are you doing here!?" it demanded. Ash jumped back, fell to the ground and then scrambled to collect Maia, which had slipped from her grip and rolled away. As soon as the robo-ball was back in her arms she leapt to her feet. "Who are you!?" it demanded again. The tall creature had long and matted reddish-brown hair that covered its body from head to toe. Ash got lost in its eyes. Or rather, its lack of eyes. Or maybe they were sunken so deep in its skull that it merely appeared to have no eyes.

"Um…I-" she swallowed. "I'm lost," she said, meaning that it was her brain that felt lost. Of all the Yule monsters she had stumbled across in her Krampus research, she couldn't recall ever reading about such a creature, which did not care for her answer. It growled as it raised its long hairy arm to strike. It swung, yet missed, as Ash had the good sense to duck and run back around the corner. The blow hit the plaster of the cottage, knocking out brittle chunks of it that fell into white dust. The creature growled its disappointment at having missed its mark and lumbered after Ash.

Jack tumbled from where he had leapt, falling past several gargoyles, and even knocking some of them from the air as he ricocheted between them. A surprised few turned and followed Jack, who managed to latch onto the twisted horn of a passing reingoyle. He swayed, dangling from the horn, trying to pull himself up onto the back of the beast, which bucked as it spiraled downward. It continued its protest as Jack stood between its front shoulders and yanked up to level out their descent—and it bucked and twisted, trying with all its might to shake Jack from his back like some demented bull at a rodeo. But Jack held firm until it finally gave up control, and then he dove for Santa. He swooped down, much like he did when rescuing Feliz, riding alongside the falling Santa, gripping his arm and swinging him onto the animal's back behind him.

Santa. Was. Stunned. "Rumpus?" he gasped, getting his bearings before letting out a hearty ho-ho-ho.

"Hang tight!" Jack hairpinned the beast, feeling his heart race into his stomach, and he climbed as several gargoyles caught up.

"We've got company," Santa observed. Jack looked over his shoulder, ripped an ornament from his sash and handed it to Santa. "What's this?"

"Pepper bomb. I think."

Santa threw the ornament, shattering it against one of the gargoyles in a stinging, ashen puff of spice. It stalled, sneezing uncontrollably as a second gargoyle crashed right into its backside. A third gargoyle crashed into the second but merely bounced off its back, tumbled through the air, and latched onto Santa's head. The reingoyle they rode upon whipped about as Santa attempted to shake the gargoyle—cracking his head side-to-side while trying to pry its chubby claws from his hair. How they bounced about through the air in the most inglorious fashion! (Unless bull-riding is your kind of fun, which, in that case, it was truly glorious.) Santa pressed down upon Jack's head with one hand to steady himself, and he reached back for the gargoyle with the other. At last, and much to Jack's relief, Santa finally grabbed the little demon by the scruff of its neck, shook it furiously a few times for good measure, and pitched it aside.

"Candi!" Jack called, diving towards the jail to where Candi and Kevin urged the last of the Naughty kids into the sack.

Candi looked up, wincing at their approach with a reingoyle/gargoyle horde swarming above. She looked down, grimacing at Krampus and the troll horde thumping up from below. "Oh!" she nudged the last kid along, a little too aggressively. "Hurry! Hurry! Hurry!" The boy tripped and stumbled and slid deep inside as Candi cinched the sack shut and thrust it into Kevin's hands. "Do. Not. Let. Go!" Her eyes frowned for emphasis. She climbed onto Noxen. "Hop on!" As soon as she yanked up Kevin, they shot away, joining Jack and Santa in a race back up to Kevin's fireplace.

"Ash!" Jack shouted.

"Ash?" Santa asked, quite perplexed, scanning about at all the soot and ash that filled this world. "Ash what?"

Santa would never forgive him for letting Ash explore Krampus' cottage, Jack thought. But he couldn't just leave her here! "I-" he began, scanning about for the girl, trying to muster the courage to explain himself. But, just then, Kevin shouted.

"We got trouble!" Kevin was looking back to where Krampus and the trolls raced up the path. A reingoyle head-butted Noxen from behind, tumbling the reindeer and flinging Kevin through the air. The Goth-kid shrieked for help in a manner that normally would have found him rather welcoming his imagined death, but as he quickly had learned, his potentially real and imminent death was truly something to shriek about! Yet, despite fearing said real and imminent death, Kevin kept his focus more on scrambling for the sack of Naughty kids that had slipped from his grip. Jack corkscrewed downward to fetch the sack as a tribe of gargoyles closed in on it. Jack charged into them, scattering them with blows from the meat tenderizer and catching the sack.

"Oh," Jack groaned, looking apologetically at the meat tenderizer, handing the sack to Santa.

"I think we can overlook that," Santa winked. "Given the circumstances." He flung the sack over his shoulder and scanned about. "Such as they are."

Candi and Noxen shook off their dizziness as Jack and Santa whizzed toward them. "Can you make the jump?" Jack asked Santa.

"A few feet more." Santa carefully climbed onto the reingoyle's back, again smushing Jack's head for balance and support. He teetered as they approached, finally leaping over into Kevin's spot on Noxen's back.

Candi gritted her teeth, casting desperate side glances to where Kevin continued to tumble upward. "I told him to hold on."

"Jackie will get him!"

Ash had already done several laps around the cottage and was out of breath. As hard as she tried to put some distance between her and the creature, it was no use. She couldn't outrun the beast. Krampus was surely going to be furious at all the missed blows it dealt trying to clobber her and instead smashing the cottage. "Jack!" she screamed hoarsely, hoping he could hear…but she was so breathless that her desperation drowned out the message that felt as if it pierced the back of her throat.

This pass around the cottage, she decided to run through the sorta-garden rather than around it, hoping for a shortcut, and she gasped and winced as the prickly fruits scratched up her legs. The creature howled with the vine and spiky fruits tangling in its hair, slowing it down just enough for her to put a little space between them. And when she rounded the corner again on the front side of the cottage, she ripped open its wooden door and dove inside, scrambling to hide around a half-wall in the entryway. She peeked around the wall, catching a glimpse of the monster lumbering past the door, then passing the opening from the other direction and ultimately deciding she must have disappeared down the path into the forest.

"How am I going to get back home?" she asked, perhaps more of a prayer or a wish that someone else would find her way.

"Kevin!" Jack called, gargoyles closing in as the Goth-teen continued to fall up. He tossed him the meat tenderizer, and Kevin fumbled but finally made the catch after it had bounced from hand to hand. As he first swung, however, Kevin had started to fall and Jack miscalculated. Jack rushed past him, crashing into and scattering the gargoyles like a bowling ball to a stack of pins. He once again did his hairpin trick, but rather than catching Kevin and swinging him onto the reingoyle, Kevin merely crashed onto the back of the beast.

"Ow!" Kevin groaned, hands going to his crotch, feeling as if he had just been kicked there with the force of a thousand kicks.

"Eee," Jack winced, feeling Kevin's pain. "Sorry about that."

They charged past Noxen, to where Krampus was now perilously close to the fireplace. Santa handed the sack of Naughty kids to Kevin. "Get the children safe!"

"Yes, sir!" Jack shouted, racing away.

"And, Jackie!" Santa called. "Don't let that beast through!" The last of the reingoyles trailed after Jack. Santa turned to Candi. "We need to buy him a dash of time." Candi swooped around, veering down on Krampus and the trolls. Krampus swatted at them and missed as trolls scattered, some falling over the cliff.

Jack landed at the fireplace and hopped off, yanking the Santa sack from Kevin and swinging it at the last of the reingoyles on his tail. The Naughty kids inside grumbled with the blow that knocked the enemy out of the air. Jack pitched the sack through the flames and urged Kevin to step through the fire so he could get back to battling Krampus. He hit the reingoyle on the rump, sending it galloping away down the path and charging towards Krampus.

"You're coming with me, right?" Kevin pleaded.

"I have to help Candi." Yes, he needed to help Candi, but he was more panicked about finding Ash.

"But Santa said-"

Jack pointed at the backside of the fireplace as he marched back toward the battle. "Get the children safe and don't let the beast through. That's what Santa said!"

"Please!?" the child pleaded. For in this moment, Kevin very much felt like a child. Jack stopped, mid-step. Compassion grabbed hold of him. His shoulders relaxed. This was the tough Goth-kid. The boss of everyone. Saying *please*. He must be scared, Jack thought. Or, he learned a lesson. Maybe both. He gently nudged Kevin through the flames and into Kevin's living room. Kevin clutched the sack of Naughty kids in one hand and gripped the meat tenderizer with the other. Jack thought that Kevin looked like a human version of himself, but a terrified version now that Kevin realized the sum of all that he had just experienced. "You're safe here. You're home." Kevin didn't look convinced, as a bit of shock took hold of him. He visibly started to tremble. "I promise you, Krampus is too busy to come back for you."

Torn between doing the nice thing and doing the naughty thing, and knowing he had to get back to Ash, Jack realized he had to do the nice thing—in the most naughty way possible. He hit Kevin with a sleep-ball to put him out of his misery. The boy fell backward, collapsing onto the sack that acted like a protesting beanbag chair, bumping about underneath his weight. "I'm sorry," Jack whispered, knowing Kevin wouldn't ever hear the apology. And, again, the apology was sincere, despite Santa being right in that Jack always seemed to be saying he was sorry for the things he had done. "I have to go and find Ash before it's too late." He stepped back to the fireplace.

"Ho! Ho! Ho!" Santa called as Noxen dived again and absorbing all light. Hell briefly went dark before icy silver beams shot from Noxen's eyes, bowling over the trolls, the troll-horde scattered again. Furious, Krampus kicked a troll over the ledge and resumed his race towards the fireplace, where Jack stepped mid-way through the flames.

Noxen looped, diving into the fire and slamming into Jack. Noxen, Candi, Jack and Santa charged through the fireplace in a puff of red and green light, tumbling across the living room floor. As Santa tumbled, he shot an ice-blue light from his palms towards the fireplace. "schließe die Tür!" he shouted. The flames froze blue, and Krampus' face slammed into them from the other side.

"No!" Jack shouted as he rolled into the far wall. He popped up, seeing the magic doorway shutting and trying to catch his bearings. *What to do?* "I need-"

"They won't learn!" Krampus growled, pounding against the ice flames. "You take those kids and they'll be right back on the Naughty list next year. You'll see!"

Santa looked outside and back into the fireplace. "It's almost sun-up. Sure you want to continue this?" To which, Krampus yelled in frustration. "Maybe next year?" he jabbed.

Candi's jaw dropped. "Are you seriously antagonizing him?"

Santa shot her a look, but relented…Candi was right. "Hey, Krampus?" His nemesis paused. "Crusty says hey." And then the strangest thing happened. As Krampus thought about Crusty, his demeanor changed. His rage subsided and he cocked his head askew. He smiled and bowed, much to the surprise of Jack, Candi and Santa. "Um…he also said something about biscuits and tea?"

"Krampus," the Christmas demon paused again. "Would like that. And, Kringle? 'Til next Christmas." His sinister laugh crescendoed and then faded as the ice flames melted into nothing.

Jack stared at the rather normal, boring, dormant fireplace, wondering just how he was going to get Ash back. How could he explain himself to Santa?

Santa rolled over to his feet. "Hoo, wee! Haven't felt this alive in…years. Though don't tell The Missus. She'll think I'm looking for trouble."

Candi shook Kevin's shoulder. "What happened to Kevin?"

"I dosed him," Jack said, absent, still staring at the fireplace, trying to remember the words Santa used to open the portal. Kevin groaned and rubbed his head as he rolled off the sack of Naughty kids. "Micro-dosed. I guess."

"Magic's wearing off," Santa explained. Crusty?!" he called. "A little help? Again?" The white wisps swirled in as Santa spoke at the ceiling. "I told him you said hey. Probably should have opened with that." A much older-sounding *Ho-ho-ho* chimed from the space about them, and Santa, appreciating the sound, let out his own hearty *Ho-ho-ho*. Aside from a sack full of Naughty kids needing to be home, Christmas would be okay.

Jackie, of course, knew that wasn't quite exactly true. And seeing Santa in a good mood for the first time in a long while made it that much harder for him to explain there was still a Naughty kid trapped in Hell. And that he left her there.

# 16 – SANTA'S SECRET

Ash stared outside to where the monster had disappeared down her path, wondering what to do. Had she waited long enough to safely follow behind? Would Jack be able to find her? She knew she had been in this place before. Not in the cottage, but however vaguely, being in this place last Christmas Eve. How did she get home from there?

All she could remember clearly—relatively speaking, anyway—was that, along with the other Naughty kids, she felt different about something. Something specific. A bit of trouble she got into when she was still friends with the Goth-kids. This was way before the block party fiasco. The pig. Yes, it was the pig! Of course, she didn't forget the pig incident but just remembered that that was what had brought Krampus to her house. Last Christmas, anyway.

On the morning of the pig, boys from the basketball team were bullying Micha on the bus. The Goth-kids banded together to stand up against the team but knew that a direct assault would find them getting their butts kicked. Horribly. Later, while dissecting a pig during their Biology class, Ash casually observed that the lab was right over the cafeteria table where the basketball team ate.

A plan was hatched.

At lunchtime, the Goth-kids all snuck away to the empty lab, tied a rope around the legs of a dissected pig, and threw it out the window. They intended to merely lower the pig, dangling entrails and all, outside the lunchroom window to gross out the team, but in their haste to pull off their prank and make a clean getaway, they had miscalculated. The rope was too long. The throw had too much momentum. The pig swung out, crashed through the screened window of the cafeteria, snapped from the rope, and slid across the table where the team ate.

Not only did this create a mess of loaded lunch trays that had tumbled onto the basketball team, but when the boys saw what caused the commotion, many of them vomited straight away, which spread like a contagion across the room. Why were we always making people sick, Ash wondered, thinking back. The animal's small intestine had flung out and draped itself across the team captain's chest, who looked down at the fleshy coil in horror and attempted to scramble away backward from himself at a fever's pace. He tripped on the bench and then slipped (on said contagion) and broke his arm in the fall, thereby getting benched for the remainder of the season.

The Goth-kids weren't ever caught, and Ash didn't exactly feel bad about the incident. She just felt that it had gone too far, which was how many of the group's antics went. She didn't mean to, but Ash pulled ever so slightly away from the gang. She found herself just a little "too busy" to hang out as much as she usually did. This greatly offended Kevin, who then booted her from their clique completely.

Even then, Ash didn't feel bad about what they had done…not even a little bit…until she found herself in Krampus' Hell and had the full realization of what she had done. Surely the gang was all there with her last year. But she couldn't remember them being there. All she could really remember was that she began to feel differently inside. Sorrowful. That perhaps she deserved to be punished. And then, somehow, she was home again.

Had the Goth-kids woken up and looked outside, they would have seen the most peculiar sight in their cul-de-sac…but they didn't wake up. Crusty had taken good care of them and made sure they were resting well after their blows from Krampus. Outside in their cul-de-sac were two teams of reindeer, two sleds, a couple of elves, Santa, and a much more humbled version of their very own Kevin. It was just before dawn, and the crisp air filled with countless stars like an abundance of Christmas wishes—twinkling, expectant, full of hope and dream.

As a Naughty kid stepped from Jack's sack and climbed into a second sack, Santa surveyed the sky, looking eastward and habitually checking for the time on a watch he wasn't wearing. "Okay, let's get these children home before sun-up. Jack, you're with me. Candi, you take the other team."

Kevin tugged at his sleeve. "Can I help?"

"Sorry, son," Santa nodded, just as Candi tugged at his other sleeve, urging him down to speak in a hush.

"It will do him good to help," she insisted.

Santa winced. "But then we'd have to circle back."

And then Candi's big eyes grew even bigger, all doe-eyed. "Please? I could use the help."

Santa sighed, feeling irked and hurried. "Fine."

"And, Santa?" she added. "Can I please take your team instead?"

And then…The Santa Look. He put so much effort into that frown. "Nobody rides Santa's team except Santa! How hard is that to understand?" And when she flashed her doe-eyes again, he snapped. "No! Don't make your eyes all bubbly like that." But for a moment he reflected on the night he had and her part in it all, and he relented again, but only a little. "But maybe…maybe I can make an exception and let Rudolph lead your team." Candi's appreciative smile slipped out a giggle, just as Santa threw a playful glare at her. "Seeing as how you've been taking him out for joyrides."

Her face twisted up…busted. "I think," she paused, considering an apology. "I think I'm good with Noxen."

Santa looked down with a slight smile. "Thank you for teaching me a lesson about him," he said. "He's brilliant."

Candi turned her attention to Jack. "Am I going to see you later?" she asked, and Jack paused. This seemed to be the oddest question to him. "You've met Krampus," she explained, "so the whole perma-swear thing…"

"Oh!" Jack shook away his confusion. "I do not want to live with Krampus. Definitely."

"But that doesn't mean you want to come home."

As Candi was perhaps the only one at The Pole who could possibly understand him, Jack grew sad. Why was it so hard for her to understand? "I don't belong at The Pole, Candi." He twisted away from her disappointment to hop into Santa's sleigh, pausing a moment to pat himself down as if he had forgotten something. "One moment."

Santa rolled his eyes. "The sun won't wait for you, Rumpus."

But Jack had already darted back to Kevin's house. He peered inside the front door and called out in a hush. "Crusty? Can you help me?" His eyes darted about the space of the room, scanning for any sign that the old elf had heard him. "Can you open the door to Krampus?" More expectant looks met with more desperate nothing. "Snowballs!"

Ash finally felt safe and desperate enough to step outside the cottage. She peered across the rocky yard and as far down into the path as she could to see if there were any signs of the lumbering monster with no eyes. She couldn't see him, but she did notice something else. The sky had grown less cluttered from reingoyles and gargoyles. The paths upward overflowed with trolls scampering downward. The battle cries had subsided. The battle was over. "Oh, no!" She scanned about for Noxen zipping above, but nothing. Did Jack win or lose? Was Kevin okay?

Instinct moved her, and she started out towards the path, but when she saw the first sign of trolls returning to the cottage, she dove back inside and slammed the door shut. And locked it. And fretted about what the heck she was going to do next.

Crusty was no longer using the snow globe to watch over Kevin's house. Hearing that his old friend was up for biscuits and tea, he turned his gaze into the underworld. How he missed his friend. How much regret twisted at him that he wasn't ever able to save Krampus from himself. The Doctor Jekyll version of Krampus—the one that most resembled his dear friend—was nearing the cottage amid the dead forest, surrounded by his minion trolls, who at once reveled in their proximity to their Christmas demon, and yet remained ready to scamper away should his darker Mr. Hyde escape him. Which was bound to happen.

And it did happen. Krampus took one look at his beat-up cottage and howled his anger. The trolls scattered in fear as he bound three and four strides apiece, looking about for whoever dared damage his beloved home.

"Oh, my!" Crusty gasped.

Krampus surveyed all the holes on the front side of his cottage and turned the corner to see his garden now a disaster. Another howl seemed to echo across every rock cliff in the underworld. He continued about his house this way—inspecting the damage and howling his rage that grew so powerful that the fog inside the globe vibrated.

"Oh, no!" Crusty gasped again, holding his breath as he peered through the fog. He flicked his ancient and bent hand across the globe's surface to shoo away the fog and get a better view of what he thought he saw. What he had hoped he wasn't seeing. "No, no, no, no, no…" He could see Ash dart from window to window, peering out in fear, looking like some trapped and frightened animal. Another howl sent shivers down Crusty's spine as he hopped to his feet. "Gah!!!" he shouted and sprinted off as fast as he could through North Pole Headquarters.

Like Candi, Santa grew sad upon hearing Jack lament about not belonging at The Pole. And with that sadness returned his grumpiness…so much so that Jack and Santa's ride together remained silent, with Jack constantly dodging his side glances as he worried about what to do about Ash.

"Now you're all grumpy-face again," Jack observed, at last.

"Randy Jones," Santa nodded. Jack hopped to his feet and called into the sack for Randy, helping the boy climb out a moment later. "How do they get home?" he finally asked Santa. Just maybe, he thought, his problem would work itself out and he wouldn't have to make Santa any more disappointed in him than he most certainly already was.

Santa grunted at the oddity of the question. "Uh…we're taking them home."

"No, I mean…if the Naughty kids were still with Krampus. How do they get home?"

"You're still bent on that demon?" Santa snapped.

"I'm not bent on Krampus!"

Their exchange made Randy uncomfortable, and he took to watching the blur of houses scroll below him so as to pretend he wasn't there in the sleigh with them. Christmas songs and stories were nothing but jolly; certainly not full of Santa bickering with elves.

"I could have gotten them all out, quietly," Santa grumbled. "If you would just do what you're told."

"I didn't *ask* you to go and rescue Candi," Jack snapped. "What I asked for was for you to just open the door to Krampus!"

"Don't! Just don't!" Santa glared. "I didn't want your help!"

"But you needed my help!"

"Only because you helped me in the first place!"

Jack stood on the seat, defiant as ever. "Only because, *once again*, you didn't give me what I wished for!"

Santa mocked him through gritted teeth. "Well, maybe we're too much alike in that we don't care what other people want!"

"But-" Jack thought, starting to chuckle. "You're Santa." And then Santa got to thinking on the absurdity of their arguing, and he chuckled too. Jack sat down again. "Being nice is so freakin' hard."

"No, Jackie," Santa sighed. "Being nice isn't hard. Doesn't make it easy just the same. Just be mindful."

"It was all my fault."

"And yet, it wasn't all your fault. Yes, all these Christmases your wish has been to meet Krampus, but there was more to it, wasn't there? Something I just couldn't give you."

Jack thought. "To run away from The Pole?"

"Nobody is a prisoner at the North Pole. If you want to go, then go, but I can't give that to you. That's something you need to take."

"I don't belong there."

"The North Pole is your home, Jackie. Of course, you belong there." Santa paused on his words, biting his lower lip. "More than you can fathom." Randy grimaced…okay. Santa nodded back to him, telling Jack it was time.

"Randy Jones," Jack said. He thought back to his first house. "Randy Jones!" And then further back to the night at the post office. "Ah! Randy Jones!" Santa and Randy Jones didn't know what to make of Jack, who put up a finger and instructed Santa with a "Wait up!" He looked into his sack and reached about, shooing Naughty kids out of the way. "Where is it? Where is it?"

Guessing what Jack was thinking, Santa whispered so no one else could hear, "Kommensiefür Randy Jones." And with that, a toy whizzed through the sack and smacked into Jack's palm.

"Gah!" Jack winced at the sting, pulling out his toy robot.

Santa looked over through a side glance. Randy's eyes grew wide. "Decimator!" he shrieked, snatching it from Jack's hands and hugging it tight. Jack's delight only gave way when he saw Santa's subtle disapproval…and when Randy's eyes grew sad, realizing. "But," he said,

"I'm on the Naughty List." He held the toy at arm's length, fighting to keep it, urging himself to give it back to Jack. Jack looked to Santa with pleading eyes…can I give it to him? Santa sighed, rolled his eyes and nodded…whatever.

"You can keep it," Jack insisted.

Wide-eyed, Randy darted between the two…really? But he couldn't keep it. That was part of his lesson. He pushed it back to Jack. "Maybe next year."

Jack took the toy back, disappointed. "Okay, then." He grabbed Randy by the shoulders and held him over the side of the sleigh.

Of course, Randy protested. "Wait-what?!" He kicked and squirmed and tried to reach out for the safety of the sleigh. "Santa!"

And Santa's response was also not the hearty *Ho-ho-ho* of Christmaslore. Instead, Randy got a half-hearted "Be nice, kid. Ho-ho-ho."

Jack dropped him over his house as Randy's shouts of terror gave way to hooting. Pastel-colored sparks flew out and ignited a twisting-turning water-slide-like path downward. Enshrouded in the sparkling light, Randy laughed, zipping down towards his house. He passed through the roof as if he were a falling angel, slipping through walls, studs, wires, and pipes, and finally flashing through red and green sparks through the STAR WARS poster on his bedroom wall. He slid through and into bed, already asleep. But moments later, he awoke, looking at his wall as if remembering. He rolled over and knelt before the poster, feeling it as if expecting it to be something other than a poster.

Perfectly normal. "What a weird dream," he thought, before realizing…It's Christmas!

Ash snuck from window to window, frantic and trapped. Krampus and trolls surrounded the house…though the trolls were keeping a safe distance from their leader, whose anger raged in deafening cries. She kept wincing and covering her ears with each howl, the worst of which came when Krampus found that someone had locked him out of his own home.

There was no escape, Ash feared. Best she could do, perhaps, was hide and perhaps sneak away at night. Did this place even have a night? She hurried through the kitchen and dining area, scanning about for a hiding spot when she spied a large cupboard that had ornate scenes hand-carved into it. Winter scenes. Scenes of Krampus and Santa enjoying each other's company in a simple sleigh, being pulled along by a team of not reindeer, but horses. She paused on the vintage picture that hung from its side—the black-and-white photograph that had been painted over with color. A jovial and slightly troll-like motley crew. She took the picture from where it hung and looked into the faces, tracing a curious finger across the surface of the picture.

The commotion outside jerked her attention, and she haphazardly re-set the picture before swinging open the heavy wooden doors and climbing inside. She crawled to the back of the space, hiding behind jars of pickled veggies, bottles of Plumberry Wine, snacks and tea.

Her heart pounded in her ears. Her breath sounded unnaturally loud. She dripped with sweat. "Calm down, Ash!" she admonished herself, and her robot spheres chittered their reassurance. She patted them gently, hushing them. And focusing on keeping them quiet relaxed her mind just a tiny bit, but only so long as she didn't worry about finding her way home.

Now, Crusty wasn't the young elf he once was. He didn't move as fast as he wanted, and he needed to take breaks on his sprint toward the old Workshop. He'd plop down on a stack of copy paper reams to catch his breath and remind himself how forgetful he could be. "Ashanti Omondi," he'd repeat to himself. "Ashanti Omondi." As his racing heart would calm, he'd look about the dark office space of Headquarters. "Ashanti Omondi." He needed a stray reindeer. Or maybe a Kettlekart. His days of running were well behind him, let alone doing all-out sprints like this. "Why am I even running?" he asked himself, trying hard to remember, and when "Ashanti Omondi" randomly escaped his lips, he sprang to his feet. "Oh!" he ran towards the Workshop. "Ashanti Omondi!"

The pastel beams shot out from Santa's and Candi's sleighs as more children slid home. Kevin watched the world blur by. "How do you see anything?" Candi peered over the edge…the world looked perfectly normal to her. She shrugged his thought away just as she tried to shrug away her sadness. "Hope," Kevin reminded her. "Right?"

She smiled a sad smile at him, thoughtful, but nodded in agreement. "Hope."

From a distance, it looked as though swirling pastel beams shot out from the sleighs rapid-fire at the houses below. But Polar Magic moved time normally inside the sleighs.

Santa began a confession of sorts. "When I saw you were readying to run away, I knew this had to be the year you finally met Krampus."

"You knew?"

"I expected you'd jump all over the *Ride With Santa* contest, but when you didn't bite I honestly thought your plan was to steal Rudolph. I really didn't want you running into Krampus on your own."

"So you canceled Christmas," Jack said, flatly.

"The Missus gave me an idea. If I canceled it, I could better see what steps you'd take. Like stealing the Naughty List." He flashed a mocking frown that didn't quite form The Santa Look.

"I didn't actually steal it," Jack began but stopped on Santa's fake cough. He sighed, as busted as Candi.

"And then you—or Candi—got Christmas uncancelled. I threw caution to the wind and made a plan that would only work if you thought it was your plan working against me."

Jack shook his head. Embarrassed. Ashamed. Why couldn't he just do the right thing? "I'm sorry."

"It's okay. All part of the plan."

"To meet Krampus?"

"Oh!" Santa beamed, the rosiness of his cheeks burning brighter than Jack had seen in a long time. "So much bigger than that, Jackie!" He nodded, "Amy Doohan."

Jack looked inside the sack. The last of their Naughty kids. He helped her climb out, and she gave Santa the biggest hug. "Thank you," she said, sincerely.

"Thank Jackie," Santa winked. She wrapped her arms around Jack for the biggest bear hug, like he was one of her stuffed toys. Initially taken aback, Jack returned the hug, with intense joy and love overwhelming him. Santa smiled, appreciating the moment, knowing that Jack was the right choice.

Jack wiped away a stray tear, leading Amy to the edge of the sleigh. "Be good, kid."

At last, Crusty had reached the old Workshop, and he paused in front of its wide glass window. He took in the displays of old toys and hand tools, the Santa sack ready to be stuffed with toys from the toy hopper. It was all so much simpler back then, he thought. The toys. The children. The holiday. All so much simpler.

He thought back to his days working in this place. The smell of pine wood. Sneezing at sawdust. His hands cramping as he chiseled away when carving a doll's face, painstakingly making the details symmetrical. Going home at the end of the day covered in paint. He put his hand to the glass, lost in his memories of his simpler days until, quite unexpectedly, he blurted, "Ashanti Omondi."

"Gah!!!" he jumped, and sprinted out into the cold, to the snow-covered path to his cottage.

Throughout the Underworld, Krampus had a reputation for having, shall we say, anger issues. The trolls, who both idolized and feared their leader, remained hidden at the dead-tree line, watching Krampus do laps about the cottage, noticing ever more damage and growing angrier and angrier. He repeatedly returned to his front door and shook its knob, seemingly expecting the door to magically unlock itself since the last attempt. And each time the door failed to open, he'd howl and stomp, shaking the ground and accidentally causing more plaster to break from his walls. The trolls all wanted to help him, to do something to help him simmer down. When one particular stomp had caused a window to shatter, Krampus shrieked in such a way that his noise, echoing from cliff to cliff, caused rocks to break free and tumble about them. Krampus shook the doorknob again, but instead of lashing out with a howl and a stomp, this time he ripped the door from its frame and threw it into the yard. As soon as he retreated inside, the trolls all scampered from the trees and set to making the repairs needed to please their Krampus.

Krampus paused to collect himself now that he was inside his home. His home that someone broke! His home that someone had locked him out of! He took in a deep breath; tried to still himself out of fear of destroying his personal space.

"Whoever you are," he taunted, initially planning to add his usual *you've been naughty!* But, that didn't feel appropriate here. He wasn't set on teaching this vandal a lesson. He wanted revenge. He felt so violated that someone would trash his home! His garden! His…another deep breath. He stretched and cracked his neck, and noticed a smear of blood across the floor. "You hurt yourself," he finally added.

Inside the cupboard, Ash gasped, trying to bend her leg in the cramped space to see how badly the prickly fruits had scratched her up. She caught glimpses of Krampus from between where the cupboard doors met, as he passed this way and then that way, following a trail of blood droplets that led from one window to the next, until finally, the cupboard shook from him slapping his hand against its side. "Hmm…" he growled, his nails scratching against the wood. She heard the picture being straightened just before the sliver of light that came in from between the cupboard's doors got blighted out. Krampus stood just inches before her. Oh, this adventure was not supposed to play out like this. The doors tore open and Ash did her best to push herself further backward, as far as she could push herself as if she could flatten herself like a pancake against the back wall.

Krampus peered between the jars and boxes and bottles, moving from shelf to shelf. Ash knew she was only seconds away from getting caught. But, just as he reached the second shelf just above her, a hand reached out from the blackness behind her, covering her mouth as another phantom hand grabbed her by the collar and yanked.

As if she was pulled through some dark tunnel, Ash tumbled backward from Crusty's cupboard and fell onto his cottage floor. He slammed shut the cupboard doors and sighed the biggest sigh of relief, just before the loudest cacophony of Christmas bells jingled and the Northern Lights shimmered brilliantly, illuminating The Pole in a bright, eerie, greenish-yellow glow that caught everyone off guard. Even those who had been celebrating a little too much at The Nutcracker Tavern found themselves suddenly sober and alert.

Ash cowered from the noise as Crusty remembered— only two kinds of folks exist at The Pole; those who belong there, and those who are invited. "Welcome! Welcome!" he shouted. "You are most welcome at the North Pole!" And with that, the bells subsided, the Lights shimmered back to normal, and the festivities resumed. Ash took in her new surroundings, stunned into silence.

"You're hurt," Crusty observed and rushed outside to the snow.

"A monster was chasing me," Ash said, empty.

"Krampus, no doubt." He returned with a handful of wilted leaves mixed with slushy, glowing snow, which he smeared onto her leg. The icy mess turned dark and thick when it mixed with the soot and dirt on her leg.

"Ah!" she winced from the cold until her leg numbed and healed. "And no. I mean, yes. Krampus, yes. But, no, it wasn't Krampus." Yanked from dripping sweat to having the frigid air of The Pole wafting over her found Ash trembling uncontrollably. Crusty wrapped her in a blanket and rubbed her shoulders. "It was hairy. Had no eyes."

"Hmm," Crusty thought, fixing her some tea and bringing her biscuits, which she devoured quickly.

"Careful, careful. Don't burn yourself. Where did you meet him? This monster?"

"I got Maia from Krampus' house, and was running back to the path." She sipped some tea. "He surprised me when I came around the corner."

"Karakoncolos," Crusty thought.

"Kara-?"

"-koncolos. Turkish. He hides around corners and then jumps out at you." Crusty startled Ash by absently lunging forward. "Oh, sorry…he asks you a seemingly harmless question and your response has to have the word *black* in it. Or else."

Ash frowned. "That's…weird."

"Much of our world is weird. But, here we are. Might you be feeling well enough to walk?"

She nodded as he helped her to her feet. "There was also Mary Lywd." Crusty looked confused. "*The* Mary Lywd. Ghost horse. Not just some horse skull on a stick."

"What would they both be doing in Krampus' realm, I wonder." Crusty looked up to Ash, took her hand in his and patted it. "But you're safe, now, Ashanti Omondi."

"Ash."

"Ash it is. Come along." He led her out into the cold, still wrapped in his blanket. "It's a short walk, I promise."

Candi and Kevin re-approached the cul-de-sac, having delivered the last of their Naughty kids. "This has been fun," Kevin smiled.

"You've got a weird sense of fun, kid. There's your house."

"I'm going to forget all this, aren't I?"

"I hope not." Kevin climbed onto the edge of the sleigh, the wind tousling his long black hair. "Be nice, Kevin."

He teetered on his balance but turned back a devilish grin. "No promises. But I'll try."

"Well, if you can't be nice, then make like an elf."

He hopped off with a laugh. Candi smiled, rushing to the edge to watch his descent, and for a moment she considered the rules…Naughty or Nice? Naughty or Nice? And, like Jack, she knew the difference between the two, and yet somehow they at times were the same thing. She tossed something into the pastel light that wound its way into Kevin's bedroom. In a flash of red and green, Kevin slipped through the wall and into bed, asleep. And, like Randy, and much of the other Naughty kids, he woke up, looking about with the strangest sensation of having forgotten something. *It's Christmas!* He thought it nothing more special than that, as special as that was. He felt something under the covers. He reached under the blanket and pulled out the oddest surprise…a meat tenderizer. But how did that get there, he wondered. Had he been sleepwalking? He thought some more, curious. And more thinking as random thoughts and images of his adventure popped in and out of focus in his mind, and then…a huge smile. It really was Christmas!

Indeed it was, or very nearly it was, for the Chicago suburbs anyway. Up in the sky, Jack flashed one last sleep-ball. It shot up, glowing, sparkly-wet. And as the sun peeked over the horizon, the snowball melted into a wet nothing.

"I'm going to miss that," he said. "As lame as it is."

Santa and Candi's sleighs met and then headed up high into the sky, back towards The Pole.

Ash stared into the wide window of the old Workshop. "That's where it all happens, huh?" It seemed so small a place to her, certainly smaller than one might expect.

"Used to be," Crusty corrected her. "Back in my days, this is where we made the toys. Nowadays we've got a huge Toy Shoppe factory that can turn out all sorts of crazy gadgets. Nobody wants just a simple wooden train anymore," he lamented, leading her into the old space. Crusty appreciated how fascinated Ash was, running her hands along the long wooden table, and picking up a hammer that was so tiny in her hand. "Krampus is right about a few things," he finally said. "Christmas used to be so very simple."

"He used to ride with Santa?"

Crusty smiled. "Yes, back when he was more like himself."

"He had a picture on his cupboard. I think it was the Yule Lads."

Crusty's smile stretched into an ear-to-ear grin. "Oh, that's wonderful." He nodded, without offering an explanation. "That makes me happy." He nudged her towards a ladder that led up to the second floor where ancient toys were mounted to appear as if floating in the air and falling into a large hopper that funneled the toys into a Santa sack. "You're going to need to help me up. I'm not as spry as I once was, you know."

Ash started to climb. "What are we doing?"

"Got to get you home."

"Oh…" She eased herself onto the second-story floor and reached for Crusty. "Couldn't I stay here?" she asked. And, upon seeing his shock, she quickly added, "I mean, for a few days maybe?"

"No!" He climbed to his feet and brushed the dust off his pants. "Your parents would worry, and that would lead to questions and questions to problems, and no…sorry."

Ash nodded in agreement, though that didn't ease her disappointment any. "Well, how is climbing up here going to get me home?"

"Ashanti Omondi-"

"Ash."

"Ash. You are truly a gift to this world. And right now you need to act like one." Ash twisted her face, perplexed. "Close your eyes and listen to my words." She complied. "You are a gift. Recognize the joy and love and light you bring." It was a nice thought to Ash, yet felt a little moonie. "Imagine that light welling up inside you. Your joy and love are overflowing. Can you imagine that?" She nodded, keeping her eyes closed as he led her to the edge of the hopper. Had she opened her eyes, she would have seen the light Crusty was referring to. Ash glowed as a strange, tingling sensation radiated out from her heart and down to her toes, up through her hair, and shooting sparks from her fingertips. Crusty gently nudged her into the hopper, and like the many gifts to the world that used to come from this Workshop, Ash slid down and into the Santa sack at the end of its funnel.

Jack, of course, didn't know that Ash was at The Pole, safe with Crusty, and his conscience weighed heavy upon him, but before he could confess to leaving her in Hell and trying to ask again if his problem might somehow resolve itself or if he needed to go back and get her, Santa continued his own confession.

"I wasn't always Santa, you know."

Jack considered that with a twisted face. He always knew Santa's name was Kringle, but he never imagined Kringle as anything but Santa. "Guess I never really thought on it."

"When I was chosen, I was an elf not much unlike yourself. *Fly for Santa* was the perfect opportunity to see who might just become the next Santa." His eyes arched, a touch of his old tiredness returning. "I'm about ready to pass on the reins."

Wide-eyed, Jack reached for the leather straps. "Really?!"

Santa smacked away his hand. "No! Not now!"

"Oh."

"But soon. Becoming Santa brings changes. You get tall. Age differently."

"And you get fat?" Jack smiled.

"Yes," Santa mocked. "You get fat. Though I reckon that has more to do with cookies. Crusty chose me-"

"Crusty?!" Of course, Crusty! Jack thought. No wonder he was so ancient. No wonder he was so tall. He must have been Santa before Santa was…Santa. Oh, he felt overwhelmed. Mind. Blown. Overwhelmed.

"He chose me," Santa paused, hesitant, seriously making sure, and sure he was right. "Much for the same reason I'd like to choose…you." Jack blinked, silent. Santa nodded with a look to ensure that Jack got the point. "I've been Santa for so long, nobody remembers Crusty was the one before me. Except The Missus, of course. You're a natural-born leader, Jackie."

"Leader?" Jack harrumphed. "No. Everyone hates me."

"And yet they follow you. Who else could have inspired a factory uprising to get Christmas uncanceled?" Jack thought…maybe Candi? But, then again, Candi tended to operate in the shadows. "And who else can I choose? Feliz? He's a bully. Plus, I need someone who can handle Krampus. Feliz just wet himself."

"No way!" Jack laughed.

Santa laughed with him but then grew serious. "Share that with nobody."

Jack held up a Scout's Honor salute. "Just me and Emily Dickinson."

Santa chuckled. "And nobody flies quite like you do, Jackie. Elves. They're followers. And you, and Candi, are definitely not followers. You have big hearts. You care about others, even if you go through life pretending to hate everyone and everything."

"I don't hate everyone," Jack lamented. "But I'm not so sure I can be a leader when everyone hates me."

"Well, you coming home, or should I drop you off somewhere cold, like Chicago?"

Jack thought, watching Candi fly ahead. "I don't like cold. And Santa? You don't want me. I left -"

Just then Jack's Santa sack puffed and wiggled as Ash climbed out with a start, not having expected the initial fall into the hopper, and then being magically transported across the globe. Again. "Jack!"

"Ash!" Jack cried out, practically sobbing with joy, as the two wrapped their arms around one another and squeezed, clinging to one another's soul. "You're safe!"

Santa was only mildly annoyed at having to turn back to the cul-de-sac yet again. The joy and relief Jack had at seeing her crawl from the sack brought a touch of joy to his own heart, even if he didn't understand why Jack was so happy that he cried. Jackie Rumpus was the right choice. Santa knew this. Despite all his faults, Jackie was perfect.

# 17 – ONE CHRISTMAS WISH

As Candi descended around Gumdrop Mountain over The Pole, she could see and hear the end-of-the-year celebrations continuing down below. Cheers erupted as soon as someone pointed out the occasional sparks that wafted from Noxen's eyes, and everyone scampered towards Headquarters. She landed her reindeer team and was met by some stable hands who congratulated and applauded her, which made no sense to her at all. She gave Noxen a hug and a kiss, and patted him on his side, thanking him for their greatest adventure yet. A dim flicker of appreciation returned as the stable hands led the team into the barn for food, water, and a much-needed rest.

"Don't hide him in the back!" Candi demanded, before adding…*please.*

Candi stood alone on the cold plain. The wind blew her blond hair and howled a loneliness. The shock of green had somehow faded. Maybe because the holiday was very nearly over. Maybe because the hope she had clung to had begun slipping from her grip. Whatever the reason, it no longer looked festive, and she no longer cared for the color. She looked up to the empty sky and sighed…well, that's that. She headed back to Headquarters, and as she stepped through the sliding glass doors, she was met with the most wild applause. She stood motionless, bewildered at the excitement among the throng of elves. The Missus handed her a peppermint ale as Crusty hugged her. "Merry Christmas, Candi Kane," he greeted.

"Merry Christmas," she returned, but there was no merry in her greeting. Her misplaced faith in the perma-swear failed. Krampus was indeed real! And Jackie was gone.

The Missus looked past Candi to the cold outside. "Where's-"

"They were right behind me," Candi shrugged, sipping her ale. "Until they weren't." She gulped the rest of her drink as The Missus rubbed her shoulders.

"Someone get this girl another peppermint ale! She's earned it. Going up against the likes of Krampus? Saving the children?"

Crusty squealed with delight. "Did you see the way Jack caught Santa?"

Now, Candi was even more bewildered. "How did you see-"

"You two are heroes!" exclaimed The Missus.

"I don't feel like a hero."

Crusty smiled. "A quality among true heroes."

Santa barged through the doors and another wave of excited cheers rolled through Headquarters. "Ho! Ho! Ho! Merry Christmas!"

"Welcome home, Kringle," said The Missus, greeting him with a hug and kiss. Candi saw him alone and felt simply crushed with defeat.

"Kringle!" Crusty looked about. "But, where's Jackie?"

Santa threw a smile to Candi, along with a wink. "Someone tripped over a saddle in the reindeer barn."

The doors opened, and Jack stumbled in, sneezing uncontrollably. "Stupid saddle!" More sneezes. "Stupid pepper bombs!"

"Pepper bombs went off," Santa beamed.

Candi was all smiles, just as Jack was all sneezes. "Snowballs!" he sneezed. "Stupid-" Another sneeze. Jack saw the crowd and then stifled yet another sneeze, acting cool. "I mean, whatever." He nearly jumped back outside when they all cheered for him.

Candi rushed him for a hug. "Jackie! You're home!"

He was taken aback by the hug. Taken aback by the cheers. By the crowd...looking at him. By how the weight of their looks felt so heavy and yet so light at the same time as if something had changed in them, and maybe something had changed in himself. They were looking at him, and they saw *him*. Past the eyeliner, and past the pale makeup, past the Goth clothes and into his heart. They saw him. Just *Jack*. This was the complete opposite of everything he always said he wanted, and yet he knew, that this was exactly what he always really wanted. He dug deep into his pocket and presented Candi with her jack-o-lantern bat necklace. The one made festive with a Santa hat. "I wanted to give this to you. Again."

Candi took the necklace and held it close. She wanted to smile. She wanted to cry. She looked to Santa with heart-happy gratitude…she got her one Christmas wish.

Crusty patted Jack on the shoulder. "Welcome home, Santa."

The greeting surprised Jack and confused Candi. Jack looked up to Santa…huh?

Santa nodded. "If you choose to be."

Crusty clapped, and the crowd clapped with him. The applause grew, as did the cheers, such that several days later, Jack could still hear it ringing in his ears. He felt home, finally. Like he belonged at The Pole.

Overlooking the Toy Shoppe factory, Jack stood on the catwalk with Candi, Santa and The Missus. He tore off a sheet from the *Days To Christmas Eve* calendar and shouted out. "Okay, gang! Only three hundred and fifty days 'til next Christmas Eve!" He turned slyly towards Santa. "Let's have some fun!" He cranked up the holiday music—which was festive, but with an angsty Goth-band twist. And he danced, not caring that the entire factory floor of elves watched him dance. Candi joined in the dancing as Santa and The Missus laughed in appreciation.

Throughout the ranks of the elves on the factory floor, some were dressed with hints of Jack's style—jet black hair there, dark eyeliner there, a few piercings scattered about. But none was as inspired as Feliz—who wore the dark eyeliner, and had the fake piercings, and had dramatically etched along the back of his work vest *RUMPUS*.

Feliz rolled his eyes, watching his new-found hero dance above them. "Whatta freak!"

The End.

# ABOUT THE AUTHOR

John Rae is a produced screenwriter and author who enjoys writing about misfit characters and their misadventures. He lives in the Chicago suburbs, where he is pretty sure Krampus has paid a visit or two. You can learn more about his projects at JohnRaeWriter.com.

For updates and previews and the occasional freebie, please visit JohnRaeWriter.com and sign up for the newsletter.

# COVER ART

Alison Anderson was born and raised in a small town in the Midwest, just down the river from our storied town of Algonquin. She attended the American School of Neon in Minneapolis, studied Illustration and Commercial Art, and is a certified welder.

Alison has been commissioned for sculpture, line drawing and logos. Her current focus is on marker art, upcycling, and illustration.

You can find more of her work at JohnRaeWriter.com/AAnderson.

Bitter wind swirled through the cavern as the troll trekked inside, creating an eerie howl that sounded both empty and yet hiding something. A distraction, maybe? Gully shook off his paranoid thoughts, knowing it was too soon to be afraid. To be *this* afraid, anyway. Twisted candelabras hung upside down along the winding walls that narrowed as he moved deeper into the cave, and from those dangled grýlukerti, icicles that glowed dim and blue to light his way. He snapped one from its base to bring its light closer.

Something inside the burlap potato sack slung over his shoulder began another round of protests. Kicks and grunts, followed by a frustrated scream that was muffled by a mouth stuffed full of a dirty sock. Another howl grabbed Gully's attention, and his thick gray beard scratched across his shoulder as he snapped his head towards the cave opening. "Quiet, you!" he grumbled in a whisper. His prisoner complied, but not before giving another swift kick to Gully's back. He gave his paranoia another listen, just in case. His eyes blinked in the blue light of the icicle he held in front of him, fear taking his breath. And he listened until he realized he was merely waiting for his imagined stalker to materialize until he could hold his breath no longer and he finally took in a deep raspy gasp. He closed those steely eyes and mumbled to himself. "Almost there."

The kicks and grunts resumed as he stomped down the path. In olden days, that sack might be full of Naughty children, being brought home for Mother to cook up into a stew for him and his brothers. But they don't eat children anymore. Gully and his brothers don't, anyway. No, what struggled in his potato sack was something not nearly as tasty when stewed like a Naughty child. This tasted gamy and somewhat pickled. He only knew as much on account of the year that Iceland simply had no Naughty children to eat. Mother rounded up whatever she could find to cook for their post-Christmas Yule Feast, perhaps thinking that none of her sons would notice any difference. And she might have gotten away with the swap, chalking up the poor-tasting meal as simply being due to a bad crop of Naughty kids, but she made the mistake of letting a few wings simmer into the stew.

That was the final year that the family held their Yule Feast with Mother. Absently picking a Zephyr's wing from his teeth was disgusting enough, but something about eating an elf felt too close to home for Gully and his brothers. For most of his brothers, anyway. It felt wrong. Poor taste aside, it felt like eating family. Mother, of course, didn't have any issues with that, having eaten two of her husbands and countless suitors. But, for her sons, well, the meal left a poor taste in their mouths that time itself hadn't been able to wash away.

And that got the brothers to thinking…elves felt like family. Not family like the siblings they were to one another, but family like the ones you choose throughout your life. Randos that stumble into your life and, for no reason at all, quickly occupy a large space in your heart to the point where you can't ever imagine they weren't always there to begin with, and you would simply die to keep them around. And for as tasty as child stew was, certainly, a Naughty child occupied someone's heart the same way.

The dim light melted within his grip, seemingly dripping a path for him to follow, and he moved the light up and down the wall as he walked along, until he found a wide crack that hid tucked behind a large, pointed, gnashing jaw of stalactites and stalagmites. He hung the struggling sack atop a short stony branch and untied it so that a head wriggled and poked through. A Zephyr. He craned his neck, rubbing his forehead against the opening to brush away the disheveled blond hair from his eyes, which were normally a rather mellow shade of brown, but seeing as how they were all he had to communicate his anger with, they now shimmered with furious speckles of gold. He grunted and shouted his protests, again still muffled with his mouth stuffed shut.

Gully scratched the end of his bulbous nose, trying to determine the best course of action here. "Zephyrym," he sighed, forcing a smile. "Friend."

The elf's eyes frowned as he bobbed his head and shouted some more. It had never been considered fashionable for Zephyrs to sport facial hair, but this particular elf opted for a perpetual five o'clock shadow that, in the days since his capture, had grown into an uneven, haggard beard that looked downright squirrelly. *Pickled*, Gully cringed. Zephyrym—Z, as his friends called him—had considerably ripened since they drank together a few days before in some pub near Dalvik.

Gully's fake smile turned into a grimace, a pleading expression that unfortunately looked threatening. Trolls can look downright menacing even at their most jovial, even one such as Gully, who—huge nose aside—appeared more squattish-human than troll. "Are you ready to be reasonable?"

A few more shouts followed by a grunt and silent pout was the answer Gully needed. He paused, reaching for the sock only to remind the elf to be quiet, which got a narrowing of the elf's eyes in response. Gully tugged at the sock, surprised and apologetic for how packed it seemed to have been shoved into the elf's face. And, once removed, the elf took a deep breath and yelled. "Friend?! You shove a rank sock in my mouth for days on end? Friend?!" He coughed and rolled his tongue across the roof of his mouth, trying to work up some saliva to spit out the foul taste.

"Hush! Shh…shh…shh…" The troll looked about towards the howls coming from the cave entrance, slapping his hand over the elf's mouth, but not before the elf bit him good, drawing blood. Gully winced from the pain. "You are in danger here!" he shouted in a hush. "Please be quiet!" He removed his hand.

"Only in danger 'cause you dragged me here!"

"I have more unsavory clothes I can shove in your face if you don't pipe down." The elf turned away with a disgusted huff. "Z, I'm sorry. I really need-" Gully paused, dodging to put himself into the elf's line of sight. "Would you at least look at me?" But the elf twisted away. Gully stepped around to look him square in the face and Z bent his neck so that he sorta turned away and sorta looked up and then backward as if he were trying to stare straight into the stalagmite that held up the sack in which he dangled. Gully straightened up and looked down at the pathetic elf who had contorted himself into the most awkward position. "Now, you're just being ridiculous."

"I'm ridiculous?" Z now looked at him, keeping his tone to a hush. "Just days ago I was chugging ale with someone I thought a friend. And now I'm tied up in a sack, dangling from a rock. Yeah…I'm ridiculous." He had finally managed enough saliva and spit at the troll's feet.

"I captured you," Gully said flatly as if that explained their predicament.

"We were drinking-"

"Until you had a few too many and then passed out," Gully paused. "And then I captured you."

"You didn't capture me!" He wriggled in his protest.

Gully flashed his eyes wide and turned his head about as if telling the elf to consider the words that had recently tumbled from his own mouth. "I need you to deliver a message."

"Why didn't you just ask?!"

"I did. And you said no."

"You did not," the elf insisted.

"You were a bit inebriated when I asked. But let's pretend that that never happened and I asked you just now for the first time to deliver a message, you would say-"

"No!"

"Exactly!" Gully caught his breath, realizing the decibels of their chat were starting to escape them. "So I had to capture you. Rules of Engagement. You're a Zephyr. Now you have to deliver the message."

"That sounds patently racist."

"You are magically bound to deliver my message. But like a captured Leprechaun who is magically bound to take you to his pot of gold, you will lie, and cheat, and manipulate, deflect, and do whatever you can do to convince me that I do not *want* you to deliver my message."

"Zephyrs *and* Leprechauns? You're on a roll." He looked at the cave floor about his feet. "Racist."

"I do not have time for this, Z." Gully tugged at the neck of the sack so that the elf could twist out. "And I'm already so very late."

"You broke my wing!" the elf complained.

"It's only sprained."

"How would you know?!" Z darted at Gully, poking him in the nose.

"Because it's flapping. You're flying. You're fine. I really am sorry, Z." He shook his head, pointing to the set of clear, insect-like wings; one of which was slightly bent, but working. "I'm desperate."

The elf hovered before him, pouting. "Say please."

"Please."

Z crossed his arms across his chest, making a show of scratching out the dirt under his nails by using his thumbnail. "Pretty please."

"Pretty please, with sugar on top, strawberries and whipped cream. For the love of Pete, I know you can't help yourself, but please stop with this and just help me."

"I can't help myself? Because I'm a-"

"Zephyr, yes. And I'm the most racist troll of all time. As a matter of fact, trolls are a pretty racist race. We can't help ourselves either. So try to forgive me the way I try to forgive you and can we *please* just get on with it!"

The elf sighed. Racist or not, the troll was right. Rules of Engagement and all. Z couldn't help himself but to simply fight what he knew he was magically bound to do. Perhaps it was part of the original spell that cursed all Zephyrs.

"I will make it up to you," Gully pleaded, looking skittish toward the cave opening. "I promise. We'll share a whole barrel of rum!"

The elf had one last impulse. "So I can pass out and you can-"

"Capture you?" Gully's thick wiry eyebrows arched up in question.

Z put his hands on his hips. "What's the message?"

Gully broke another glowing icicle off a candelabra and pointed it into the crack in the wall. "I need you to retrieve it."

The elf cocked his head towards the crack, insulted. "Zephyrs don't *retrieve* messages. Nor do we deliver packages! Fetch it yourself."

Gully patted his belly. "It gets narrow in there. I've put on some weight since I was in there last."

"And you got cheese growing in your beard," he frowned.

"I…wha-?" He brushed his fingers through his beard to find crusty milk leftover from the pail he pilfered at the barn where he last crashed for a night. "I'm saving it for later."

"Get one of your gangly brothers to fetch for you. I'm not your dog. What's his name?" Z snapped his fingers. "The sheep guy."

"Stekkjarstaur."

"Your family has issues."

"Don't they all? Look, the brothers know nothing about this, and for now, I need to keep it that way. Now, I know you're upset with me-" He waved his hand at the elf, speaking over his interjection. "And rightfully so! Again, I'm sorry. Truly. And I could have just captured any Zephyr or hired anyone to take up this task. But the reality is, Z, I *trust* you. And I really need someone I trust." Gully watched the elf hover a bit, listening to the wind drown out the flapping of his wings. He waited for another snarky comeback. Another distraction. Another protest. But, instead, Z snatched the icicle.

"Fine!" the elf snapped. "What am I looking for?"

"You'll know it when you see it."

Z's shoulders rounded as if his arms suddenly felt heavy, skulking the way a teenager might as they storm off to their room. He entered the crack in the wall, accidentally rebounding against its side.

"Still a bit hung over, are we?" Gully grinned.

"My wing is broken!" Z snapped back, mocking Gully as his light disappeared into the crack. "Still a bit hung over, are we, blah blah meh meh meh."

Just then, one of the things Gully had feared had started to appear. A dark shape passed along the upside-down candelabras as it made its way down the corridor. Gully tensed up, surprisingly thankful that this wasn't even the thing he was most worried about.

"Quiet!" Gully whispered, breaking another icicle from the wall. "Stay hidden." He pointed the glowing spear towards the cave entrance, where a large set of glowing, yellow-green, feline eyes rounded a corner and blinked. An overgrown feral cat lumbered into his space; taller than Gully and just as haggard. Its whiskers twitched, bent and broken, likely from its latest battle with some Naughty child. Always hungry, it sniffed in Gully's direction, the ends of its long fangs exposed.

"Go home, cat," Gully warned, nudging the animal with the pointed ice. It purred, hardly bothered or interested in him, for it didn't care for the taste of troll, just as the troll didn't care for the taste of elf. But, unlike Gully, an elf would satisfy the cat's hunger for a lack of Naughty children. And it smelled something pickled. "There are no Naughty children here."

The cat made little jabbing motions about Gully's head as it sniffed for the elf's whereabouts. It brushed past him towards the crack in the wall, earning an icy jab under its ribcage. "I said go home, cat!" It seized up, arching its back to make itself appear even larger than it unnecessarily was and raised a paw with claws exposed, ready to swat the troll. But Gully didn't back down. He couldn't back down!

The cat had a taste for Naughty children, but it had the most peculiar way to discern Naughty from Nice. If a child had been gifted with a new piece of clothing for Christmas, it deemed the child *Nice* and would pass on the morsel. But, if the child had not received any new pieces of clothing—a scarf, a hat, socks, anything!—it had found its next meal. But, of course, not first without tormenting the sad child the way a normal housecat might play with a mouse, or a bird, or some other unfortunate plaything.

And that's the part that worried Gully, for even though he knew that he wasn't a tasty treat for the cat, he understood that the cat liked to play, and maim, and kill. Although the cat stood taller than him, and its raised paw was wider than Gully's head, the troll admonished the beast the way a smallish parent might threaten a large, misbehaving child that could easily beat their parent senseless. Of course, only Naughty children would think to do so. Gully remained stern, and with authority, he commanded the creature once again to go home. The cat hissed, narrowing its glowing eyes, and obeyed. It slunk around, snaking its tail along Gully's neck as it turned and strutted back up the path toward the cave entrance.

Moments later, the elf zipped past Gully. "I ain't gonna forgive you this." Z listed a bit to the right, which Gully initially thought was due to the weight of the small velvet sack he carried, but then he realized the sprained/broken wing wasn't fluttering with the others. It merely twitched, quite randomly, and all too slowly.

"Is it the wing?" the troll asked, apologetic.

"Ya think?" he frowned so hard that his eyes nearly disappeared from the bend in his brow. Gully watched him try to hover still, but he kept veering askew. "It really stings." He rolled his shoulder like one might after sitting hunched over a desk for too long.

Gully wondered how that might help the wing at all. *What it must feel like to have wings*, he thought, *let alone a broken wing. It was probably just sprained*, he tried to convince himself again. "You can get that to Kringle, though, eh?"

"What?! Hailbunk! No wonder I said no. Kringle? Last time I had to deliver a message that way, I got nearly trampled before they welcomed me and turned off the blasted bells!"

Gully thought a moment. "You've been there before? You think maybe you'd *still* be welcome there?" The question was as much about Z as it was about himself.

"I don't right know the ins and outs of Polar Magic."

"Hmm…" Gully frowned. "Well. We'll find out, won't we?" He took Z by the arm and put his other hand around the elf's back, carefully navigating around the flapping wings, and turned him towards the cave entrance. "Just show him the message. You'll be quite welcome, I'm sure." He gently nudged him away as the elf mocked him for a goodbye.

"Just show him the message!" Z made the most gravelly, troll-like voice he could manage as he flittered up the path.

Gully winced as the elf bounced against the rock wall. "And be quiet!" he snapped. "That cat might still be around."

"And be quiet," the elf repeated, in a not-so-quiet tone, disappearing around the bend. "Blah blah blah blah blah."

Gully sighed, waiting for the sound of an elf getting eaten by a cat, but only after first getting tortured. But no such sounds were heard, and Gully momentarily relaxed, but not before wondering if maybe the cat could have been stealthy enough to take his friend quietly. "Nah!" He dismissed his paranoid thought, turning towards the depths of the path toward home. To his brothers.

He didn't want to face them. To lie to them, if that was necessary. Or explain why he missed their brothers-only Yule Feast, which would certainly be necessary. He thought about these next moments the entire journey home, and yet, he still didn't quite know what to say to them. How would he convince them to sneak away from Mother? To go on a dangerous journey behind Z? And probably do battle with an elf they would surely rather avoid? And that would be only if the ogre didn't catch up to them first.

That Jackie Rumpus was training to become the next Santa was no secret in their world, yet there were many secrets swirling about this news. But there was a most important secret that Gully had to break to his brothers. A secret that would affect them greatly.

*Jackie Rumpus could not become the next Santa!*

Jackie's misadventures will continue in *Bad Elf and The Kristkindl*. For updates and previews and the occasional freebie, please visit JohnRaeWriter.com and sign up for the newsletter.

# ONE LAST WISH

One of the best (and most appreciated!) ways to help an author is by leaving a review. Doing so feeds the internet algorithm monster, which then helps other readers find this story.

Please feed the beast by leaving a review at JohnRaeWriter.com/reviews!

Much thanks and love,

John